Penguin Books
Friday, or The Other Island

Michel Tournier was born in Paris in 1929, but spent much of his youth with relatives near Dijon. This, his first book, won the *Grand Prix de roman de l'Académie Française*, and his latest book, *The Erl King*, won the *Prix de Goncourt*.

Friday
or *The Other Island*

by Michel Tournier

Translated from the French
by Norman Denny

Penguin Books

Penguin Books Ltd, Harmondsworth,
Middlesex, England
Penguin Books Australia Ltd, Ringwood,
Victoria, Australia
Penguin Books Canada Ltd,
41 Steelcase Road West, Markham,
Ontario, Canada
Penguin Books (N.Z.) Ltd,
182-190 Wairau Road,
Auckland 10, New Zealand

First published as *Vendredi, ou les limbes du Pacifique* by
Editions Gallimard 1967
This translation published by William Collins, London
and Doubleday, New York 1969
Published in Penguin Books 1974

Copyright © Editions Gallimard, 1967
Copyright © English translation
William Collins, Sons & Co. Ltd, and Doubleday & Co. Inc., 1969

Made and printed in Great Britain by
Hunt Barnard Printing Ltd, Aylesbury, Bucks
Set in Intertype Baskerville

Il y a toujours une autre île.

JEAN GUÉHENNO

Prologue

With the precision of a leadline the lantern hanging from the cabin roof measured by the extent of its swing the roll of the brig *Virginia* in a sea that was growing steadily worse. Captain Pieter Van Deyssel bent forward over his stomach to place the tarot-pack on the table in front of Robinson.

'Cut and turn up the top card,' he said.

He lay back in his chair and puffed smoke from his china-bowled pipe.

'So it is the demiurge,' he said. 'One of the three major fundamental arcana. The picture shows a tumbler standing at a bench scattered with miscellaneous objects. This means that in you there is an organizer, one who does battle with a world in disorder which he sees to master by whatever means come to hand. He appears to succeed, but we must not forget that the demiurge is also a juggler: his work is an illusion and his order illusory. Alas, he is unaware of this. Scepticism is not his strength.'

A heavy thud shook the ship and the lantern made an angle of forty-five degrees with the roof. The *Virginia* had suddenly swung so that she lay almost across the wind, and a wave had crashed with a sound like cannon-fire on to the deck. Robinson turned up the next card. It depicted, smeared with splashes of grease, a crowned and sceptred figure standing upright in a chariot drawn by two horses.

'Mars,' said the Captain. 'The little demiurge has achieved a seeming victory over Nature. He has triumphed by force of will and imposed an order which is in his own image.'

Crouched like a Buddha in his chair, Van Deyssel gazed at Robinson with eyes twinkling with malice.

'An order in your own image,' he repeated thoughtfully. 'Nothing so gratifies a man's soul as his belief that he has the power to impose his will without restriction. Robinson the King ... You are twenty-two. You have deserted – that is to say, you have left behind in York – a young wife and two children, to seek your fortune in the New World, like so many of your compatriots. Later they are to join you – if God permits. Your close-cropped hair and square, russet beard, your clear-eyed, steady gaze, in which there is a hint of something narrow and rigid, your attire, whose sobriety is near to affectation – all this puts you in the happy category of those who have never had doubts. You are pious, parsimonious and pure. The kingdom over which you will preside will be like one of those great tidy cupboards where the women of our country keep their piles of immaculate linen scented with lavender. You must not resent these remarks. You need not blush. What I am saying would be mortifying only if you were twenty years older. The truth is that you have everything to learn. Stop blushing and turn up another card ... What did I tell you? That is the Hermit. The Warrior has become conscious of his solitude. He has withdrawn into the depths of a cave to seek the wellspring of his life. But in doing so, in burying himself in the bosom of the earth and exploring to the depths of himself, he has become another man. If ever he emerges from his retreat he will find that his monolithic soul has been intimately fissured. Draw another card.'

Robinson hesitated. This bulky Dutch Silenus, lapped in a luxuriating materialism, was saying things with decidedly uncomfortable undertones. Since taking passage in the *Virginia* at Lima Robinson had contrived to avoid any close contact with the devilish man, having been soon put off by his dismaying perspicacity and cynical epicureanism. It had needed this storm to make him in some sort a prisoner in the Captain's cabin, the only place in the ship where any shred of comfort remained; and Van Deyssel seemed resolved to make the most of the chance of amusing himself at the expense of his simple-minded passenger. When Robinson refused a drink he had produced the tarot-pack, and now – while the storm thundered in Robinson's ears like the din of a witches' sabbath accompanying the unholy game in which he was obliged to take part – he was richly indulging his gift of prophecy.

'Well, here's something to bring the Hermit out of his hole! Venus, no less, rises from the waters and takes her first steps on your drab earth. May I have another card? Aha, Sagittarius, the sixth Mystery. Venus, become a winged angel, shoots arrows at the sun. Another, please. Oh, dear! You have turned up the twenty-first Mystery, that of Chaos! The Beast of the Earth is in conflict with a monster of flame. The man you see, caught between opposing forces, is a clown, recognizable by his cap-and-bells – or at least he will become one. Another card. Well, this was to be expected. It is Saturn, the twelfth Mystery, depicted as a hanged man. But what is significant about the figure is that, as you see, he is hanging by his feet. You are head down, my poor Crusoe. Another card quickly! It is the Twins, the fifteenth Mystery. I was wondering what would be the next avatar of our Venus transformed into an archer. She has become your twin brother. The Twins are depicted attached by the neck to the feet of the bi-sexual angel. Take particular note of that!'

Robinson's thoughts were wandering. Yet the groaning of the ship's hull under the battering of the waves was not causing him undue alarm, any more than the reeling flight of the scatter of stars visible through the skylight above the Captain's head. The *Virginia,* an unhandy ship in light airs, was at her sturdy best in heavy weather. With her

9

stubby, unraked masts and short, beamy hull of 250 tons she looked more like a floating washpot than a greyhound of the seas, and her lack of speed was a subject for jesting in every port she tied up in; but her crew could sleep soundly through the roughest gale, provided she was not on a leeshore. To this might be added the temperament of her skipper, who was not the man to affront winds and tides or run undue risks for the sake of holding his course.

In the early evening of 29 September 1759, when the ship was in the 32nd parallel of the southern latitude, the glass had fallen sharply while St Elmo's fires twinkled at the ends of masts and spars, heralding a storm of exceptional violence. The southern skyline towards which the brig was sluggishly heading was so black that when the first drops of spray fell on deck Robinson was surprised to find them colourless. A sulphurous darkness enveloped the ship while a wind of gale force got up, coming approximately from the north-west, but gusting and veering through five or six points of the compass. The easy-going *Virginia* had been forced to battle as best she might with a long, deep swell that buried her bows as she emerged from every trough; but she had continued on course with a sturdiness that brought a tear to the sardonic eye of Van Deyssel. However, after two hours, a sound like an explosion had brought him running on deck to find that his mizzen had burst like a balloon and was now no more than a few shreds of tattered canvas. With honour satisfied, and feeling that he need defy the elements no longer, he had put the ship about and ordered the helmsman to hold her before the wind. It was as though the storm had acknowledged the act of surrender. Since then the *Virginia* had sailed without undue buffeting through a tempestuous sea whose furies seemed suddenly to have lost interest in her. Having seen to it that she was fully battened down, Van Deyssel had sent the crew below, excepting the helmsman, a look-out and the ship's dog, Tenn, who remained on the poop. He then installed himself in his cabin with all the consolations of Dutch philosophy – a flask of Hollands, a cheese flavoured with caraway-seed, slices of pumpernickel, a teapot heavy as a kerbstone, a pipe and a tobacco-jar. Ten days earlier a green line on the port horizon had told them that the ship, having entered the Tropic of Capricorn, was passing the Desventurado Islands. Heading south, she should on the following day have entered the waters of the islands of Fernandez: but the storm was driving her eastward towards the coast of Chile, from which she was still one hundred and seventy sea-miles distant, with no intervening island or reef, according to the chart. There was therefore no cause for alarm.

The Captain, whose voice had been drowned for some moments by the tumult, now resumed his discourse:

'We again find the Twins in the nineteenth major Mystery, the Arcanum of the Lion. Two children hold hands in front of a wall symbolizing the City of the Sun. The Sun-god fills all the upper part of the picture, which is dedicated to him. In the City of the Sun, set between Time and Eternity, between Life and Death, the inhabitants are clothed with childlike innocence, having attained to solar sexuality, which is not merely androgynous but *circular*. A snake biting its tail is the symbol of that self-enclosed eroticism, in which there is no leak or flaw. It is the zenith of human perfectibility, infinitely difficult to achieve, more difficult still to sustain. It seems that you are destined to rise even to these heights, or so the Egyptian tarot-cards say. My compliments, young sir.' Rising on his cushions, the Captain made Robinson a little bow of mingled irony and deference. 'But may I have yet another card? Ah, it is Capricorn, the door which is the soul's way out – that is to say, death. The fateful tale is told clearly enough by the skeleton mowing a meadow planted with hands, feet and heads. Flung down from the heights of the City of the Sun, you are in grave danger of death. I long to see the card which follows, and I dread it. If it is a weak symbol your story is done . . .'

Robinson was now straining his ears for something else. Had he not heard, mingled with the grand cacophony of wind and sea, the sound of a human voice on deck, and the barking of a dog? It was hard to tell, and perhaps he was too preoccupied with the thought of the look-out man, exposed to all the fury of that hellish storm. The man was so securely roped to a stanchion that he might have had difficulty in releasing himself to give the alarm, or have feared to do so. But would his voice have been heard amid the tumult? Had he not cried out just now?

'Jupiter!' exclaimed the Captain. 'Jove! Robinson, you are saved, but at the very last moment! You were falling like a plummet, and the great god has come most expeditiously to your aid. Here he is, in the guise of a golden child, issue of the entrails of the earth, like a nugget from a mine, restoring to you the keys of the City of the Sun.'

Jove . . . Was not that the word Robinson had heard amid the roar of the tempest? Jove . . . But then he realized that it must have been a sound resembling it, the syllable 'ho'. That was what the man on deck had shouted, what any look-out must have shouted, catching a brief, terrifying glimpse of an unknown, uncharted coastline – 'Land-ho!'

'All this may seem to you a meaningless farrago,' resumed Van Deyssel. 'But it is a part of the wisdom of the tarot-cards that they do not predict our future in precise terms. Think of the dismay if they did! They do no more than afford us, at the best, an intimation. My brief lecture is in some sort a coded message, and the key to the cipher is your future itself. Each forthcoming event in your life will in its occurrence reveal the truth of one or other of my predictions. Prophecy of this kind is not so illusory as it may at first appear.'

He drew thoughtfully at the curved mouthpiece of his long-stemmed Alsatian pipe. It had gone out. Getting a penknife out of his pocket, he scraped the dottle from the china bowl into the scallop-shell which served him as an ashtray. Robinson, still intently listening, heard no more human sounds amid the tempest. The Captain opened his big tobacco-jar by means of the leather tab fixed to its tight-fitting wooden lid, and carefully inserted the pipe in a trough scooped in the tobacco which nearly filled the jar.

'Thus it is secured against shocks,' he explained, 'besides being impregnated with the honeyed scent of *Amsterdamer*.' Then, become suddenly motionless, he looked hard at Robinson. 'Crusoe,' he said sternly, 'take heed of what I say. Beware of purity. It is the corrosive of the soul.'

At this moment the lantern, swinging with a sudden wildness on its chain, smashed against the cabin roof, and at the same time the Captain was flung head foremost across the table. Plunged into a sudden, shuddering darkness, Robinson tried to feel his way to the door. He found none, but presently a violent blast of air told him that he was in the alleyway outside the cabin. He stood trembling, afflicted in his entire body by the terrifying immobility that had succeeded the plunging movement of the ship. Up on deck, by the tragic light of a full moon, he saw a party of sailors attempting to hoist a lifeboat on its davits. He started to go towards them, and as he did so the planks were swept from under his feet. A blow struck the port side of the vessel that was like the battering of a thousand rams. An instant later a black wall of water fell with a crash upon the deck, sweeping it from end to end and carrying everything away, men and gear alike.

Chapter 1

A wave curled and running up the wet foreshore licked Robinson's toes as he lay face down on the sand. Still only half-conscious, he drew in his legs and crawled a few yards higher up the beach. Then he rolled over on his back. Black and white gulls wheeled screeching in a limpid sky where only a wisp of white, drifting eastwards, remained to tell of yesterday's storm. Robinson tried to sit up and as he did so felt a sharp pain in his left shoulder. The foreshore was littered with gutted fish, shattered shellfish and piles of brownish weed such as grows only in a certain depth of water. North and east the skyline was open sea, but to the west it was broken by a rocky promontory which seemed to continue under water in a series of reefs. It was here, some two cable's lengths away, that the pathetic shape of the *Virginia* rested, propped amid the sharp outcroppings, her broken masts and tangled shrouds a mute proclamation of disaster.

When the storm had burst upon her the ship must have been lying to the north-east of the Juan Fernandez archipelago, and not due north of it as Van Deyssel had supposed. Running before the wind, she must have been driven down on to the outer reefs of the island of Mas a Tierra instead of heading into the hundred and seventy miles of open sea which separated that island from the Chilean coast. This at any rate was the theory least unfavourable for Robinson, since Mas a Tierra, described by William Dampier, was populated by people of Spanish extraction, rather thinly scattered, it was true, amid the forests and grasslands of its sixty-odd square miles. But it was also possible that the Captain had made no mistake in his reckoning, and that the *Virginia* had run aground on an uncharted island somewhere between Juan Fernandez and the American continent. However that might be, he must set about looking for other survivors from the wreck, and for inhabitants of the island, if such there were.

Robinson got to his feet and walked a few paces. No bones were broken, but his left shoulder was badly bruised. Fearing the intensity of the sun, which was high in the sky, he fashioned a conical hat for himself out of a frond of the ferns which grew thickly between the beach and the edge of the forest, and picking up a fallen branch to serve him as a walking-stick he entered the thorny undergrowth at the foot of the volcanic upland, from the crest of which he hoped to be able to survey the land.

Gradually the forest grew more dense. The thorny shrubs gave way to scented laurels, red cedar and pine. The trunks of dead and rotting trees lay in such confusion that at times he found himself walking through tunnels of vegetation and at other times several yards above ground level, as though on a natural footbridge. The tangle of creepers and hanging branches enclosed him as though in a vast net, and in the silence of the forest the noise of his progress was like a series of explosions. Not only did he come upon no trace of human habitation, but even animals seemed absent from the series of leafy cathedral-vistas that opened up before him. At first, approaching a motionless shape some thirty yards away which might have been that of a sheep or large goat, he supposed it to be a tree-stump, scarcely more curious than others he had passed. But as he drew near he found that this object in the green gloom was indeed some sort of wild goat, with very long hair. Head raised and ears cocked, it stood in rock-like immobility watching his approach, and he had a tremor

16

of superstitious terror at the thought that he must either walk past the weird creature or turn back. Discarding his stick, which was too light, he picked up a black and knotted cudgel of wood, strong enough to break the goat's impetus if it charged.

He stopped two paces away from it. Out of the mass of hair a single green eye with a dark oval pupil had fixed its gaze upon him. Robinson recalled that, owing to the wide set of their eyes, the majority of quadrupeds can only look at things in a largely one-eyed fashion, and that a charging bull cannot see the adversary it is charging. A strange sound issued from the hairy statue obstructing his path, a sort of belly-rumble. With fear exacerbating his state of extreme fatigue, Robinson was overtaken by a violent fit of anger. Raising his cudgel he brought it down with all his strength between the goat's horns. There was a crunching sound, the animal sank on its knees and then rolled over on its side. It was the first living creature Robinson had encountered on the island, and he had killed it.

After several hours' climb he came to the foot of a rocky mass, at the base of which was the shadowed opening of a cave. He went inside and found it to be enormous, so deep and vast that for the present he could not explore it. He left it and clambered to the top of the great pile of rock, which seemed to be the highest point of the place on which he had landed. Reaching the summit, he found that indeed he could see the whole circle of the horizon – and everywhere was sea. He was on an island much smaller than Mas a Tierra, and which gave no sign of human habitation. The strange behaviour of the goat was now explained. The creature had never before set eyes on a human being: sheer curiosity had kept it rooted to the spot. Robinson was too exhausted to measure the full extent of his misfortune. Since it isn't Mas a Tierra, he reflected simply, then it is the Island of Desolation – with this impromptu baptism summing up his state. But the sun was now sinking and he was conscious of a queasy emptiness in his stomach. Total despair presupposes the minimum of relief. Exploring the mountain-top, he found a kind of wild banana, smaller and sweeter than those of California. He dined on these, cutting them up with his clasp-knife. Then he lay down in the shadow of a boulder and fell into a dreamless sleep.

A huge cedar that had taken root by the approach to the cave rose high above the mound of rock as though it were the tutelary genius of the island. When Robinson awoke its branches were stirring in a light breeze from the north-west as though in a gesture of consolation. Its vegetable presence was comforting and might have given Robinson a foretaste of what the island could do for him, had his thoughts not been so wholly concentrated on the sea. Since this place was not Mas a Tierra, it could only be an island unknown to the map-makers, lying somewhere between the Juan Fernandez archipelago to the west, and the Chilean coast to the east. Its distance from either was impossible to determine, but both must certainly be beyond the reach of a single man on a raft or improvised canoe. Moreover, if the island was unknown this must mean that it was off the regular sailing routes.

While he reached this melancholy conclusion Robinson was studying the physical characteristics of the island. Its entire western half seemed to be covered by the dense coat of tropical forest, ending abruptly in sheer cliffs overhanging the sea. But on its eastern side there was an expanse of well-watered meadowland which turned to marsh as it approached a low-lying foreshore broken by lagoons. Only on the northern coast of the island did there seem to be a place where a boat could put in. This was a wide, sandy bay bounded at its eastern end by white-shining dunes and at the west by the reefs where the hull of the *Virginia* was to be seen, her rounded belly wedged in the rocks.

18

When finally he began to descend the hillside towards the place whence he had set out the day before, Robinson had undergone a first change. The fact of having understood and measured the solitude to which he was doomed, perhaps for a very long time, had sobered him and induced a mood of heavy melancholy. He had forgotten all about the slaughtered goat until he came upon it on his path. It was a relief to find his cudgel lying where he had let it fall, a few yards away, because half-a-dozen vultures, their heads sunk between their shoulders, were watching his approach with small, pink eyes. The goat lay gutted on the stones, and the featherless, scarlet gizzards bulging through the plumage of the carrion-birds showed that the feast was well begun.

Robinson advanced, brandishing his cudgel. The birds dispersed, running ponderously on their twisted feet, and one by one rising laboriously into the air. One of them turned and as it flew past released a green dropping which splashed on a tree-trunk near where he was standing. But they had done their work well. Only the goat's entrails, viscera and genitals, had disappeared; the rest would probably not have been edible by them except after days of baking in the sun. Robinson slung the body over his shoulders and went on down the path.

Back on the foreshore he cut off a hindquarter and roasted it hanging from a tripod of sticks tied together over a fire of eucalyptus twigs. The crackle of the flames consoled him more than the tough, musky-tasting meat which he chewed with his eyes on the horizon. He resolved to keep the fire going permanently, as much for his spiritual comfort as to save the flint and steel he had found in his pocket, or as a signal to possible rescuers. In any case, nothing was more likely to attract the notice of a passing vessel than the wrecked hull of the *Virginia*, still upright amid the rocks with its shattered masts and hanging shrouds, a melancholy sight but certain to arouse the interest of any seafarer. Robinson thought of the store of arms and provisions on board which he must try to bring ashore before another storm broke her up for good. If his stay on the island was to be a long one his survival would depend on this legacy bequeathed him by shipmates whom he must now presume to be dead. The wise course would have been to start immediately on the salvage operations, which presented great difficulties to a man working single-handed. However, he did not do so, telling himself that by lightening the vessel he would render her more vulnerable to any puff of wind and thus endanger his own best chance of getting away. The truth was that he felt an overwhelming reluctance to undertake any kind of work which would make it seem that he was settling down on the island. Not only did he cling to the belief that his stay would be short, but he had a superstitious feeling that in making any attempt to organize his life here he would be dismissing the hope of an early rescue. With his back turned obstinately to the land he kept his eyes fixed on the rolling, metallic surface of the sea, whence, surely, help must soon be forthcoming.

During the days that followed he busied himself with every contrivance he could devise for making his presence known. Hard by his permanent fire on the foreshore he collected a great pile of faggots and dried seaweed to be converted into a signal beacon if a sail showed on the horizon. Then he had the notion of setting up a mast with a cross-pole attached to the top, its longer end reaching to the ground. When the time came he would fix a lighted torch to the lower end and, pulling on the other with a rope of lianas, raise it high in the air. But he gave up this idea when, on the cliffs overlooking the western end of the bay, he found a dead eucalyptus tree of great height, its hollow trunk forming a natural chimney. By surrounding it with kindling he could rapidly transform the whole tree into a flaming torch visible for leagues around. He did not set up signals which might have been sighted when he was elsewhere, because he had no intention of leaving that stretch of foreshore, where at any moment, in an hour or two, at the most in a day or two, a ship would come sailing into the bay.

He gave no thought to his food, simply eating anything that came to hand – shellfish, coconuts, roots and berries, birds' eggs and turtle-eggs. On the third day he dragged the remains of the goat some distance away because it was beginning to stink intolerably. But afterwards he regretted doing this since it drew the attention of the vultures to himself. Wherever he went he was accompanied by a watchful escort of bleached heads and scrawny necks. The obscene creatures merely took casual avoiding action when he bombarded them with sticks and stones, as though, being the servants of death, they held themselves to be immortal.

Nor did he keep any count of the passing days, relying upon his eventual rescuers to tell him of the time that had elapsed since the wreck of the *Virginia*. So he never knew precisely how many days it was – or weeks or months – before his idleness and passive contemplation of the skyline began to oppress him. The vast, gently heaving expanse of the ocean, green-tinged and glittering, so fascinated him that he began to fear he was becoming subject to hallucinations. The first of these was his tendency to forget that what lay at his feet was a liquid mass in constant motion: he began to see it as a hard, rubbery surface on which he could walk and leap if he chose. Then, his fancy wandering further still, he came to think of it as the back of some fabulous beast whose head lay beyond the horizon. And finally it occurred to him that the island with its rocks and trees was itself nothing but the lid and brow of a huge blue and liquid eye contemplating the immensity of the heavens. This last image so obsessed him that he had to abandon his own state of passive expectation. He shook himself and decided that he must do something.

For the first time the fear of madness entered his mind. It was never again to leave it.

To do something could mean only one thing: it meant building a boat large enough to take him to the coast of Chile.

On the day he formed this resolve Robinson also realized that he must overcome his reluctance and visit the hulk of the *Virginia* in search of tools and materials useful for his purpose. With the help of lianas he lashed together a dozen dead logs to form a crude raft, which was, however, serviceable enough in conditions of flat calm. A stout pole was all the propulsion he needed, because at low tide the water was shallow until it reached the rocks, by means of which he could then manoeuvre. Reaching the wreck, which towered above him, he tied up to the stern-post and then swam round it to find a way of getting on board. There was no visible damage to the hull, which was wedged as though in a socket in a reef of low-lying rocks which were doubtless generally submerged. Indeed, if the crew, putting their faith in the ship, had stayed below instead of letting themselves be washed overboard from the deck, they might perhaps all have been saved. As he hoisted himself up by means of a rope hanging from one of the davits, Robinson reflected that he might even find Van Deyssel on board, since he had left him, injured no doubt but still alive, in the comparative safety of his cabin. Scrambling on to the well-deck, which was so encumbered with the tangle of broken masts and spars, sheets, shrouds and halyards that it was difficult to pick one's way through it, he saw the dead body of the look-out, still lashed to the stanchion on the foredeck, like the victim of an execution. The poor wretch must have been stunned by some sudden blow before he could cut himself loose, and so he had died at his post after fruitlessly giving the alarm.

The ship's store-rooms, down below, were in a similar state

of shambles. But at least the sea had not penetrated every-where, and stowed away in the lockers Robinson found supplies of ship's biscuit and salt meat, of which he ate as much as he could manage without fresh water. There were also casks of wine and stone flagons of gin, but his lifelong habit of abstinence had left him with the distaste which the animal organism in its natural state feels for fermented liquors. The Captain's cabin was empty, but then he saw the Captain lying in the navigating bay. He felt a tremor of intense delight when, as he thought, he saw the gross body make a movement, as though responding to the sound of his voice. But the bloody and hairy mass of the Captain's head was hanging limply; it had merely been shaken by a strange shudder proceeding from the torso. And as Robinson stood in what remained of the doorway the bloodstained folds of the Captain's jacket were thrust apart and an enormous rat emerged, followed by two smaller ones. Robinson turned away, reeling, to vomit on the debris that littered the cabin floor.

He had taken no great interest in the *Virginia*'s cargo. Although he had asked Van Deyssel about it soon after coming on board, he had not pressed the question when the Captain had replied in a coarsely jesting tone that he special-ized in Dutch cheese and guano, the latter resembling the former in its greasy texture, its yellowish colour and its smell. So it did not greatly surprise him when, securely lashed in the hold, he found forty kegs of black powder.

It took him several days to get this load of explosive ashore because he could only navigate his raft at low water. In the intervals he devised a covering for it, a rain-proof shelter of palm-leaves held down with stones. He also brought two cases of ship's biscuit ashore, a spyglass, two flintlock muskets, a double-barrelled pistol, two axes, a spokeshave, a hammer, a plane, a bale of oakum and a large bale of course red cloth, cheap material designed for barter with any natives

23

the ship might encounter. He got the big jar of *Amsterdamer* out of the Captain's cabin, and found it hermetically sealed with the china-bowled pipe undamaged, securely lodged in its nest of tobacco. He took ashore a load of planks torn from the ship's decks and bulkheads, and finally a Bible, which he found in good condition in the mate's cabin and wrapped in a piece of sailcloth.

And the next day he set about building a vessel which he hopefully christened the *Escape*.

Chapter 2

The high ground at the north-west of the island fell away in an easily negotiable slope of rubble overgrown with sparse shrubs to a sandy creek. Overlooking this creek was a flat clearing, about an acre and a half in extent, and near to it Robinson discovered, half-buried in the undergrowth, a long, straight, slender tree-trunk, evidently recently fallen, dry but in excellent condition, which would serve for the keelson of the *Escape*. The small plateau had the advantage of affording a view over that part of the sea whence help might come, and, further, that the hollow eucalyptus which he intended to use as a signal beacon was close at hand. Accordingly he took all his tools and materials there, having decided to make the clearing his shipyard.

Before starting work he read several pages of the Bible aloud. Having been brought up a Quaker, the sect to which his mother belonged, he had never been a great student of Holy Writ. But his extraordinary circumstances, and the chance, as though it were the direct intervention of Providence, which had placed the Book of Books in his hands as his sole spiritual sustenance, moved him to search those ancient pages for the moral support of which he was so greatly in need. And on that first day he thought that he found in Chapter VI of the *Book of Genesis*, with its account of the Flood and the building of the Ark, a clear allusion to the vessel of salvation he was about to build.

After clearing away the bushes to give himself working space he topped and tailed the trunk, leaving a central section which he judged to be long enough for his requirements. He lopped the branches off this section and then, using poles as levers and helped by the slight slope on which it lay, he rolled it on to the plateau, and, still using his axe, set about squaring it along its entire length.

He worked slowly and by rule of thumb, guided only by his recollection of visits paid as a child to a small shipyard on the river Ouse which specialized in fishing vessels, and later of his efforts with his brothers to build a rowing-boat – an attempt which they had finally abandoned. But he now had limitless time at his disposal, and inexorable necessity drove him to his task. When discouragement came near to overwhelming him he compared his lot with that of a prisoner painfully using an improvised tool to file through the bars of his cell, or striving to scratch a hole in the wall with his fingernails, and then he could feel that he was fortunate. Moreover, having neglected to keep a calendar since the wreck, he had only the vaguest idea of the passing of time. The days flowed monotonously by, each like the last, and every morning he had a sense of starting again on the day before.

Technical problems greatly troubled him. Those boat-builders on the Ouse had bent the planks for the strakes round forms, with the aid of steam; but he had no means of constructing a boiler on this scale, and he could only whittle them roughly with his axe and spokeshave. The shaping of the stem- and stern-posts proved so difficult that he had to finish them off with his claspknife. He was obsessed with the fear of damaging the original tree-trunk which had so providentially furnished him with a keel.

Seeing the vultures swoop over the wreck of the *Virginia,* he suffered pangs of conscience at the thought that he had left the bodies of the Captain and the lookout man unburied.

The horrid task of getting their bulky and rotting corpses ashore was one that he constantly postponed, and to have pushed them overboard would have been to run the risk of attracting sharks, which would then no doubt have hung about the bay hoping for further prey. It was bad enough to have attracted the attention of the vultures; they now never left him. He concluded that it would be time enough, when the rats and birds between them had stripped the bodies clean, to collect the skeletons and consign them to a decent grave. He even made a vow that he would build a chapel and there say a prayer for them every day. Since the dead were now his only companions it was right that they should have a place of honour in his life.

In all his searches he had found no screws or nails aboard the *Virginia*, and having no instrument for drilling holes he could not fix the planks together by pegging. He had to use mortice and tenon, rounding the latter in a fish-tail for greater strength. He even had the idea of hardening the fish-tails with fire and then wetting them with sea-water so that they would lodge more securely in the mortice. This constantly caused the wood to split under the influence of fire or water, but he doggedly remade them, existing in a kind of somnambulistic torpor, beyond weariness or haste.

Sudden showers and trails of white on the horizon announced a change in the weather. The sky one morning, although still cloudless overhead, had taken on a metallic tinge which perturbed him. The limpid blue of the previous days had turned leaden and colourless. Before long a coverlet of cloud, perfectly consistent in its density, stretched from one skyline to the other, and the first heavy raindrops beat on the timbers of the *Escape*. Robinson tried at first to ignore them, but he was soon obliged to strip off his clothes, whose sodden weight hampered his movements. After stowing these for shelter in the completed part of the hull he stood for a moment watching as the flow of tepid water over his body carried away its accretions of earth and dirt in little muddy balls. His ginger body-hair, now plastered down and glistening, was patterned by lines of force which stressed its animal nature. 'A golden seal,' he reflected with a faint smile. Then he made water, pleased to add his modest contribution to the downpour drenching the earth around him. He felt suddenly as though he were on holiday, and in a burst of high spirits he danced a few steps before, half-blinded by the rain and whipped by the gusts of wind, he ran to take cover under the trees.

The rain had not yet penetrated the numberless layers of foliage on which it beat down thunderously, while a heavy mist rose from the earth to be lost in that lofty vaulting. Robinson expected the rain to break through at any moment and drench him, but instead the earth beneath his feet grew increasingly spongy, although not a drop fell on his body. He understood the reason for this when he saw water running down the tree-trunks along small folds in the bark that might have been gutters expressly carved for the purpose. After some hours the beams of the setting sun, breaking through a gap between the horizon and the ceiling of cloud, bathed the island in a fiery light, while the rain still fell with undiminished violence.

Robinson's mood of childlike gaiety had soon abated, together with the kind of intoxication which had kept him working at his self-imposed task. He felt himself sinking into a limbo of despair, naked and alone in that apocalyptic landscape, his only companions two corpses rotting in a wrecked ship. Only later did he fully grasp the import of that experience of nakedness which he was undergoing for the first time. It was true that neither the temperature nor any consideration of modesty required him to go about clad in a civilized manner. Sheer habit had caused him to do so, and now in his despair he began to appreciate the value of that armour of wool and linen in which human society had hitherto enclosed him. Nakedness is a luxury in which a man may only indulge without peril to himself when he is warmly surrounded by the multitude of his fellows. For Robinson, while his soul had not yet undergone any change, it was a trial of desperate temerity. Stripped of its threadbare garments — worn, tattered and sullied but the fruit of civilized millennia, and impregnated with human associations — his vulnerable body was at the mercy of every hostile element. The wind, the thorned shrubs, the rocks and the pitiless light assailed and tormented their defenceless prey. Robinson felt that he was doomed to perish. Had human creature ever been subjected to so harsh a trial? For the first time since the wreck words of revolt against the decrees of Providence rose to his lips. 'O Lord,' he murmured, 'if Thou has not turned Thy face away wholly from Thy servant, if Thou dost not desire him soon to succumb beneath the weight of the desolation Thou has inflicted upon him, then must Thou show Thyself! Give me a sign that I may know that Thy Presence is still near me!' Tight-lipped he waited, like the first man under the Tree of Knowledge when the earth was still soft and damp after the receding of the waters. And then, though the rain beat yet more heavily on the leaves and it seemed that all things must dissolve in the mist rising from the earth, he saw taking shape on the horizon a rainbow greater and more dazzling than Nature alone could have contrived. More than a rainbow, it was an almost perfect halo, with only its lowest segment lost in the waters, radiating the seven colours of the spectrum with a sublime brilliance.

The downpour ceased as suddenly as it had begun, and in the act of putting on his clothes Robinson regained his sense of the purpose and urgency of his task. He had soon recovered from that brief but instructive moment of despair.

He was in the act of coupling a side-member into its precisely shaped socket, bearing down on it with all his weight, when he had a feeling that he was being watched. Looking round he met the gaze of Tenn, the *Virginia*'s dog, a setter of doubtful breeding but warmly affectionate disposition. It had stopped a few yards away and was observing him with ears cocked and one forepaw raised. A great happiness flooded through Robinson. After all, he was not the only survivor of the wreck! He walked towards the animal, speaking its name. Tenn was one of those dogs who have an absolute need of human companionship, the sound of a human voice and the touch of a human hand. It was strange, then, that instead of running to greet Robinson with his tail wagging he should have backed away, furiously growling, with teeth bared. He turned abruptly and bolted into the wood.

Despite his disappointment Robinson derived a pleasure from the encounter which buoyed him up during the next few days. Moreover, Tenn's curious behaviour diverted his mind from the problems of the *Escape* by giving him something else to think about. Did it mean that the terror and ordeal of the shipwreck had driven the poor beast mad? Or was he so disconsolate at the Captain's death that he could not endure the presence of any other man? But another thought occurred to Robinson which filled him with alarm. Perhaps they had been so long on the island that the dog had simply reverted to its natural, wild state. How long was it since the shipwreck? How many days, weeks, months, even years, had passed? He was assailed with a kind of dizziness when he asked the question, as though he had dropped a stone into a well and were listening in vain for it to reach the bottom. He resolved henceforth to make a notch in a tree-trunk for every day that passed, with a cross to mark every thirtieth day. Then he forgot the matter and went back to work on the *Escape*.

She slowly took shape, that of a beamy straight-stemmed craft, rather heavy and with very little sheer, about eighteen feet on the water-line. He could do with nothing less if he were to have a reasonable hope of making the coast of Chile. She was to have one mast and a single spar carrying a large loose-footed sail, easily handled by a single man and designed to make the most of the beam wind he expected to meet on his easterly coast. The mast was to pass through the forward decking and be stepped solidly in the keel. Before proceeding to lay the deck he ran his hand for the last time over the smooth and closely joined interior surface of the boat's sides, thinking happily of the beads of moisture that must appear when first she took the water. She would need to float for a day or two before her timbers swelled enough to make her watertight. The deck-planking, to be laid across the thwarts securing the sides of the hull, had alone cost him several weeks of arduous toil. But a decked fore-peak or cuddy was indispensable for the housing of his provisions. Although, if his hazy estimate was correct and the Chilean coast was less than 200 miles distant, he might hope in favourable conditions to reach it in a couple of days, he must make ample allowance for miscalculation and the vagaries of wind and tide.

Throughout his work he had been handicapped by the lack of a saw, having failed to find one on his search of the *Virginia*. It was a tool which he had no means of improvising, and it would have spared him months of labour with axe and knife. So much did the thought of this obsess him that one morning, hearing a sound which might have been that of a man sawing, he thought he must be the victim of an hallucination. Now and then there was an interval, as though the worker had paused to rest, and then, with a monotonous regularity, the sound began again. Robinson crept out of the cranny in the rocks where he was accustomed to sleep and advanced cautiously towards it, steeling himself against the possible shock of encountering another human being. He found the workman to be a giant crab using one pincer to

31

saw the end off a coconut which it held with its other claw. Up in the coconut palm, some twenty feet above ground, another crab was detaching the nuts at their stem and letting them fall to the ground. The two creatures seemed quite unperturbed by his arrival, and went quietly on with their business.

The sight of them was intensely repugnant to Robinson. He went on to his clearing, more convinced than ever that this place was wholly alien and hostile, and that his boat, so splendidly taking shape amid the bushes, was his only link with life.

Having no varnish or tar for caulking, he made a kind of resinous dressing following a method he had seen used in the shipyards on the Ouse. It entailed cutting down nearly the whole of a clump of holly-trees not far from the clearing. He then spent some weeks stripping these of their outer bark and peeling off the soft underlying pith which he cut into sections. He boiled the pith in a small cauldron he had brought from the *Virginia* until the fibrous mass was rendered down to a thick, viscous liquid, which he reheated and smeared over the vessel's hull.

The *Escape* was eventually completed, but the long tale of its building was inscribed for ever on Robinson's flesh, in the cuts, burns, scars, bruises and callouses bearing witness to that dogged and seemingly endless battle that had at last achieved its triumph in this uncouth but sturdy-looking boat. There was no builder's time-sheet, but his own body was record enough.

He started to collect provisions for the journey, but then put the task aside when he reflected that first he must launch his ship to determine her seaworthiness. The truth was that an obscure misgiving had restrained him from doing this at once, the fear of some unforeseen setback that might destroy all hope of success in this enterprise on which his life depended. He considered the vessel's possible defects. She

2

might, for instance, sink so low in the water as to be un-manoeuvrable and at the mercy of every ripple, or on the other hand she might turn turtle at the first puff of wind. His worst nightmare was the picture of her sinking like a stone directly she was put on the water, while he stood peering down at her, watching the eddying shape sink ever deeper into the shadow of those green, translucent depths.

After a long hesitation engendered by these terrifying presentiments, he finally made up his mind to proceed with the launching. It did not much surprise him to find that he was quite incapable of dragging the hull, which must weigh over half a ton, down the gently sloping grass and over the sand to the sea. But this first reverse, by compelling him to acknowledge the gravity of a problem which hitherto he had scarcely considered, threw a sudden light on the transformation which solitude was effecting in his own personality. His field of concentration seemed to be both deepening and narrowing. He perceived that he was finding it increasingly difficult to think of more than one thing at a time, and even to transfer his attention from one thing to another. He discovered that for all of us the presence of other people is a powerful element of distraction, not only because they constantly break into our activities and interrupt our train of thought, but because the mere possibility of their doing so illumines a world of matters situated at the edge of our consciousness but capable at any moment of becoming its centre. That marginal and as it were ghostly presence of things with which he was not immediately concerned had gradually vanished from Robinson's mind. He was now and henceforth surrounded by objects subject only to the arbitrary law of all or nothing, and thus it was that, being wholly absorbed in the business of building the ship, he had completely overlooked the problem of launching her. In addition he had been obsessed with the story of the Ark, which had become for him a sort of prototype of the *Escape*. Built on

3

her mountain-top, far from any seaboard, the Ark had waited for the rising waters to reach her.

The growing panic which at first he had managed to control overwhelmed him when he found that he was unable to slide rollers under the keel in the way he had seen stone pediments moved during the restoration of York Minster. The hull was immovable, and in his efforts to lever it he succeeded only in loosening one of the side-members. After three days of desperate, fruitless effort, fatigue and frustrate fury drove him nearly out of his senses. Then another possibility occurred to him, a last hope. Since he could not drag the *Escape* to the sea, he must bring the sea to her. All that was required was a canal or 'cut' driven from the foreshore through the rising ground to the place where the hull stood propped on its legs. When it flooded at high-water, he would tip the vessel into it. He started furiously digging; but then, his first ardour abating, he paused to consider the practical aspects of the business – the distance of the hull from the foreshore and above all its height above sea-level. His cut would need to be a hundred and twenty yards long and some ten feet wide, and by the time it reached its destination its walls would be more than a hundred feet high. The task was one that he could scarcely hope to complete single-handed in all that remained of his natural life.

He gave up.

The surface of thick slime, over which clouds of mosquitoes hovered, was stirred by sluggish ripples as a small sucking-pig, nothing of it visible but its speckled snout, moved to attach itself to its mother's flank. Several families of peccaries had established their wallow in the marshes on the eastern side of the island, and they lay there half-buried in mud during the hottest period of the day. But whereas the indolent sows, motionless as fallen logs, might have been a part of the landscape, their livelier young ceaselessly fidgeted and quarrelled, uttering shrill squeaks. At sunset the sow with considerable effort would heave her dripping bulk on to a tongue of solid earth while the children struggled with frantic squeals to avoid being sucked into the quicksand she left behind. The party would then move off in single file, causing a great commotion in the dried undergrowth.

And then a human form like a statue of clay rose in its turn and made its way through the reeds. Robinson could not have said how long it was since he had left his last shred of clothing on some thornbush. In any case, the thought of sunburn no longer troubled him, since his back, flanks and thighs were now protected by a thick coating of dried mud. His hair and beard were so grown that his face was almost invisible beneath their tangled mass. His hands had become more forepaws used for walking, since it made him giddy to stand upright. His state of physical weakness and the softness of sand and mud, but above all the breaking of some spring in himself, had led to his only moving on hands and knees. He knew now that man resembles a person injured in a street riot, who can only stay upright while the crowd packed densely around him continues to prop him up. Exiled from the mass of his fellows, who had sustained him as a part of humanity without his realizing it, he felt that he no longer had the strength to stand on his own feet. He lived on unmentionable foods, gnawing them with his face to the ground. He relieved himself where he lay, and rarely failed to roll in the damp warmth of his own excrement. He moved less and less, and his brief excursions always ended in his return to the mire. Here, in its warm coverlet of slime, his body lost all weight, while the toxic emanations of the stagnant water drugged his mind. Only his eyes, nose and mouth were active, alert for edible weed and toad-spawn drifting on the surface. Rid of all terrestrial bonds, his thoughts in a half-stupor pursued vestiges of memory which emerged like phantoms from the past to dance in the blue gaps between the motionless foliage. He recalled cosseted hours of child-hood passed amid the bales of wool and cotton in his father's gloomy store-room. The piled rolls were like a padded fort-ress absorbing light and sound, draughts of air and sudden movement. The close, musty air was heavy with the odours of wool-grease, dust and varnish, and also of the aromatic gum which his father used throughout the year to combat a cold that he could never shake off. Robinson had thought that he owed nothing except his russet hair to that nervous, self-effacing little man whose life was spent at a high desk poring over his account-books, and that all his other qualities came from his mother, who was a wonderful woman. The mire, by demonstrating his capacity for turning inward upon himself and withdrawing from the external world, had taught him that he had inherited more than he thought from that little draper in York.

In his long hours of cloudy meditation he evolved a philo-sophy which might have been his father's own. Only the past had any worth or existence deserving of note. The present was valueless except as the repository of memories accumulated in the past, and to add to that increasing fund was the only reason for living. In the end came death; and death itself was no more than the awaited moment when the treasure amassed in the past might be wholly enjoyed. Eternity was bestowed on us in order that we might re-live our life in death, more observantly, more awarely and more sensually than was possible in the turmoil of the present.

He was browsing on watercress in the bed of a small stream when he heard the sound of music, unreal yet distinct, like a celestial symphony, a chorus of crystalline voices accom-panied by the strings of a harp and a viola da gamba. He thought at first that it was indeed heavenly music, meaning that his life was approaching its end, if indeed he were not already dead. But then, looking out to sea, he saw the white gleam of a sail on the eastern horizon. Springing to his feet he ran to the building-yard of the *Escape*, where he had left his tools lying, and by good fortune found his flint-and-steel almost at once. He ran to the eucalyptus tree, and setting fire to a bundle of dry twigs thrust it into an aperture at the bottom of the hollow trunk. A cloud of acrid smoke rose up, but the huge conflagration which he had counted on was slow to materialize.

In any case, what did it matter? The ship was heading for the island on a course that would bring it into the Bay of Salvation. It must surely intend to anchor and send a boat ashore. Uttering demented cries, Robinson dashed madly about in search of a shirt and pair of trousers, which eventually he found stowed away under the *Escape*'s hull. Then he ran down to the foreshore, scrabbling at his face as though to remove the dense mat of hair that covered it. Swaying gracefully in the north-easterly breeze, the ship under full sail was drawing near the breakers running up the beach. She was one of those old-time Spanish galleons whose function had been to bring home to Spain the treasures of the New World, and it seemed to Robinson that below the water-line, as she heeled, her lower strakes were indeed the colour of gold. She was dressed overall, and from the head of her mainmast a double-pointed pennant of black and yellow fluttered in the breeze. As she drew near Robinson saw a brilliant company assembled on her forecastle and main deck. It seemed that some high festivity was in progress. The music came from a small string orchestra and a choir of children in white robes grouped on the quarter-deck. Men and women were elegantly dancing round a table loaded with dishes of gold and crystal goblets. No one seemed to see the shipwrecked man or even the shore, with which the ship was now sailing parallel, having altered course only a cable's length away. Robinson kept abreast of her, running over the sand, shouting, waving his arms, pausing to pick up sticks of wood which he flung in her direction. He stumbled, picked himself up, and fell again. She was now coming level with the first of the sand-dunes and he was held up by the lagoons at that end of the beach. He plunged into the water and swam with all his strength, seeing no more of the ship than her receding stern and aftercastle draped with brocade. A young girl was leaning out of a cabin window, and with a dazzling clarity Robinson saw her face. It was a very young face, tender and vulnerable, yet seeming already touched by experience, and illumined with a pale, sceptical and forlorn smile. Robinson knew that face. He was sure of it. But who was the child? He opened his mouth to cry out to her, and salt water poured down his throat. A green dusk enclosed him in which he had just time to see the grimacing mask of a small skate as, swimming backwards, it fled away from him.

A fiery column roused him from his torpor. He was horribly cold. Had the sea flung him a second time on the same stretch of beach? High above him, on the western cliff, the eucalyptus was blazing like a torch in the darkness, and he staggered upwards towards that source of warmth and light.

By a supreme irony the signal beacon that was to have shone out over the ocean, summoning the rest of mankind, had attracted no one to it but himself!

He passed the night huddled in the bushes, his eyes fixed on the pit of incandescence, shot with vivid colour, that had its opening at the base of the tree; and as the heat died down he drew closer. Not until the early hours of the morning was he able to give a name, a christian name at that, to the girl on the galleon. She was his younger sister, Lucy, who had died some ten years ago. Now he could no longer doubt that that vessel of a bygone age had been the vision of a disordered mind.

He got to his feet and stood looking over the sea. That metallic surface, glittering already under the first rays of the sun, had been his temptation, his snare and his drug. Only a little more was needed, and besides degrading him it would drive him to the depths of madness. On pain of death he must find the strength to tear himself away from it. The island lay behind him, huge and untrodden, rich with limited promises and harsh lessons. He must again take his life in hand. He must work. Without more dreaming he must consummate his marriage with solitude, his implacable bride.

Turning his back on the ocean, he picked his way up the slope of rubble, overgrown with silvery thistles, that led to the centre of the island.

Chapter 3

Robinson spent the next few weeks making a methodical survey of the island and taking stock of its resources – its edible plants, potentially useful animals, freshwater springs and natural shelters. By good fortune the shell of the *Virginia* had not been entirely demolished by the spells of bad weather during the preceding weeks, although parts of the deck and timbering had been carried away. So had the bodies of the Captain and the look-out man, and this was a relief to Robinson, although it caused him pangs of conscience. He had promised them a grave: instead, he would build them a cenotaph. He made the cave in the rocky tor at the centre of the island his general store-room, and here he transferred everything he could remove from the wreck, rejecting nothing movable, because even the most useless objects now possessed for him the value of relics, links with the human community from which he was sundered. After installing forty kegs of black powder in the depths of the cave, he brought in three chests of clothes, five sacks of grain, two baskets of crockery and table-ware, several cases of miscellaneous objects – candlesticks, spurs, ornaments, spectacles, pocket-knives, charts, mirrors, dice and so on – various jugs and drinking vessels, and a box of gear which included wire cable, blocks, lamps, marlin-spikes, fishing-line, floats and other possibly useful equipment; and finally he brought ashore a small strong-box containing gold, silver and copper coins. The few books he found on board were so damaged by sea-water that the print was unreadable, but it occurred to him that if he dried them in the sun their whitened pages might serve him for a diary, if he could find something to use as ink. This deficiency was unexpectedly supplied by a fish which was to be found in sholes at the foot of the cliffs on the eastern side of the island. The sea-porcupine, which is dreaded for its strong densely-toothed jaws and the poisonous prickles which rise along its spine when it is alarmed, possesses the curious faculty of being able to blow itself up like a ball. The air is collected in its stomach, and in this condition it swims on its back without seeming in any way incommoded by its eccentric posture. Robinson found, when he turned one over as it was lying on the beach, that anything that came in contact with the skin of its stomach, whether distended or slack, was stained a brilliant red with a remarkably lasting dye. The flesh was highly palatable, as firm and delicately flavoured as chicken. After catching a large number of these fish, Robinson squeezed the excretion from their skins into a cloth and thus provided himself with a somewhat evil-smelling but entirely serviceable red ink. He hastened to cut himself a quill from a vulture's feather, and nearly wept with delight when he traced his first words on paper. In thus performing the noble act of writing it seemed to him that he half-retrieved himself from the abyss of animalism into which he had sunk, and made a return to the world of the spirit. Thenceforward he resorted nearly every day to his journal, not to set down the greater or lesser events of the day, to which he attached little importance, but to record his thoughts, his spiritual progress, his recollections of the past and the reflections to which these gave rise.

A new life thus began for him – or, more exactly, it was the beginning of his true life on the island, after that period of degradation which he now thought of with shame and sought to forget. This explains why, having at length re-solved to keep a calendar, he was little troubled by the fact that he had no means of determining how long he had been on the island. The wreck of the *Virginia* had occurred during the night of 30 September, 1759, at about two o'clock in the morning. Between that date and the day when he first cut a notch in the trunk of a pine-tree there existed an indefinite and incalculable period of shadow and despair, and Robinson felt himself as much cut off from the human calendar as he was separated from mankind by the expanse of waters, reduced to living on an island in time as well as an island in space.

He spent some days drawing a map which he subsequently amplified and amended as his knowledge of the island increased. He decided to re-christen it, having from the day of his arrival bestowed on it the heavy and opprobrious name of the Island of Desolation. Being struck, during his reading of the Bible, by the admirable paradox whereby the Christian religion makes despair the unforgivable sin and hope one of the three cardinal virtues, he resolved to call it Speranza, the Island of Hope, a tuneful, sunny word which, moreover, evoked the wholly profane memory of a hot-blooded Italian girl whom he had once known. The simplicity and depth of his religious faith readily accepted these correlations, which a more superficial mind might have held to be blasphemous. It also struck him, poring over his rough map, that viewed from a certain angle the island resembled a female body, headless but nevertheless a woman, seated with her legs drawn up beneath her in an attitude wherein submission, fear and simple abandonment were inextricably mingled. The thought passed through his mind and was forgotten; but later he would return to it.

An examination of the sacks of grain he had brought from the *Virginia*, containing rice, wheat, barley and maize, caused him severe disappointment. Rats and weevils had eaten a considerable part, leaving nothing but the husks and their droppings, and a good deal of the rest was mouldy with damp. After laboriously separating the good from the bad, grain by grain, he found that, apart from the rice, which was undamaged but uncultivable, he had retrieved ten gallons of wheat, six of barley and four of maize. He resolved to sow it, for he attached infinite value to bread, the symbol of life, the only food mentioned in the Lord's Prayer, as he did to everything that still linked him with the community of mankind. And he felt that bread yielded by the soil of Speranza would be tangible proof that she accepted him, as he had accepted this nameless island on whose shores chance had cast him.

He set fire to several acres of grassland on a day when the wind was blowing from the west, and after breaking up the surface with a hoe improvised from the sheet of metal brought from the *Virginia*, in which he had contrived to pierce a hole large enough to take a handle, he sowed crops of wheat, maize and barley. He vowed to treat his first harvest as a benefaction bestowed by Nature – that is to say, by God – on the labour of his hands.

Of the animals inhabiting the island, the goats, which were numerous, would certainly be the most valuable if he could domesticate them. The kids were quite approachable, but the mothers resisted when he tried to milk them. Accordingly he built a fenced enclosure of saplings tied and interwoven with lianas. He drove a few young kids into this and the mothers followed. He then turned the kids out, and before long the fullness of their udders caused the mothers to welcome milking. In short, after cultivating the soil he started a dairy herd. Like mankind at the dawn of history, he had passed through the stage of hunting and gathering into that of tilling and stock-raising.

But he was still far from thinking of the island as a wilderness which he might conquer and subdue until he had made it a wholly human place of habitation. Not a day went by without some unexpected or hurtful incident occurring to remind him of the anguish he had felt when, realizing that

43

he was the only survivor of the wreck, he had felt himself the orphan of mankind. The sense of his forlorn state, although it was allayed by the sight of his tilled fields, his goat-pen, his well-ordered store-room and imposing array of weapons, brought a lump to his throat on the day when he saw a vampire-bat crouching over the throat of a kid whose blood it was sucking. The creature's taloned and tattered wings enfolded the small animal like a cloak of death as it lay trembling. On another occasion, when he was gathering shellfish on some half-submerged rocks, he was hit by a jet of water in the face. Slightly dazed by the shock, he moved forward, only to be checked by a second jet, aimed with uncanny precision. At once he was assailed by that familiar and dreaded sense of alienation, which was only partly relieved when he discovered, in a cavity in the rocks, a small grey squid which possessed the remarkable gift of being able to squirt water like a siphon in any direction it chose.

He eventually became resigned to the remorseless scrutiny of his 'governing board', as he termed the group of vultures who seemed to have attached themselves permanently to him. No matter where he went or what he did they kept him company, hunchbacked, goitrous and bald, watching and waiting – not, indeed, for his death as he had at first believed in his moments of depression, but for the edible fragments he scattered in the course of the day. But although he had perforce grown used to their presence, he found it less easy to endure their repulsive habits. Their love commerce, like that of lubricious old men, offended his enforced chastity. Filled with outraged melancholy, he watched the male, after a few grotesque skips, heavily tread the female, sinking his hooked beak into her bare, blood-red neck while their rumps came together in an obscene embrace. One day he noticed that a smaller and doubtless younger bird was being harried and ill-treated by several of the others. They pecked it and beat it with their wings, finally surrounding it and driving it against a rock. Then abruptly the hostilities ceased, as though the victim had cried mercy or in some way let it be known that it submitted to the demands of its persecutors. With its neck stretched stiffly towards the ground the small vulture advanced a few paces, stopped, and, shaken by internal spasms, regurgitated a decomposing and half-digested gob of meat, evidently the proceeds of a private act of gluttony which its companions had detected. They fell upon the nauseous mess and devoured it, jostling each other.

This occurred on a morning when Robinson had broken his hoe and allowed his best milch-goat to get away. It completed his demoralization. For the first time in months he had a relapse and yielded to the temptation of the mire. Following the track of the wild pigs leading to the marshland on the east side of the island, he returned to the swamp where he had come so near to losing his reason, and stripping off his clothes let his body sink into the tepid slime.

By degrees the nightmare of squids, vampire-bats and vultures which obsessed his mind vanished into that mephitic mist filled with the drone of mosquitoes. Time and space were dissolved, and a face appeared in the clouded sky, bordered with foliage, which was all that he could see. He dreamed that he was lying in a gently rocking cradle roofed with a curtain of muslin, and his tiny hands were all that emerged from the lily-white swaddling clothes that enclosed him. Around him a murmur of words and domestic sounds recalled the familiar setting of the house where he was born. The firm, controlled voice of his mother was mingled with the shriller, always querulous tones of his father and the laughter of his brothers and sisters. He did not understand what they were saying, or seek to understand. The embroidered veil parted to reveal the slender face of Lucy, rendered narrower still by the two heavy plaits of dark hair, one of which fell upon his coverlet. Weakness pervaded Robinson, exquisitely sweet. A smile parted his lips, amid the rotting grass and water-lily leaves. A small leech had attached itself to the corner of his mouth.

Journal

Each man has his slippery slope. Mine leads to the mire. That is where Speranza drives me when she grows evil and shows me her animal face. The mire is my defeat, my vice. My victory is the moral order I must impose on Speranza against her natural order, which is but another name for total disorder. I know now that in this place it cannot be solely a question of survival. Merely to survive is to die. It is a matter of building, organizing, ordering, patiently and without cease. Every pause is a backward step, a step towards the mire.

The strange circumstances in which I find myself must, I think, warrant many changes in my thinking, notably in respect of moral and religious matters. I read the Bible daily, and every day I lend an attentive ear to the voice of wisdom that speaks in me as it does in every man. I am sometimes startled by the novelty of my discoveries, but I accept them nevertheless, for no custom must be allowed to prevail over the voice of the Holy Spirit which resides in all of us.

Thus it is with Vice and Virtue. My upbringing taught me to see in Vice an excess and extravagance, a debauch and overflowing, to which Virtue opposed humility, self-effacement and self-denial. I find that this kind of morality is a luxury which would cause my death if I sought to follow it. My present situation requires that I should set wider bounds to Virtue and diminish those of Vice, regarding as virtues courage, strength, self-assertion and mastery over the external world. Vice is renunciation, self-abandonment, submission – in a word, the mire. No doubt this is to retreat beyond Christianity to a more ancient vision of human wisdom, and to substitute *virtus* for *virtue*. But at the root of a certain kind of Christianity there lies the radical rejection of Nature and earthly things, a rejection which I have practised to excess in regard to Speranza, and which has nearly been my downfall. I shall triumph over defeat to the extent that I am able to accept my island and cause it to accept me.

46

As his mortification at the failure of the *Escape* died down Robinson came to think more and more of the advantages of possessing a small, light craft in which he might explore those parts of the island's coast which could not be reached by land. Accordingly he set about hollowing a shell-canoe out of a pine-trunk – slow, monotonous work with an axe, at which, however, he toiled methodically for a set period every day, with none of the feverish excitement that he had brought to the building of the *Escape*. He had thought at first of building a fire under a part of the trunk, but he was afraid that the whole of it would become charred, and he merely lit a fire of kindling in the hollow he had begun. In the end he abandoned the use of fire altogether. Adequately hollowed, shaped and smoothed with fine sand, the canoe was sufficiently light for him to be able to lift it on his back and carry it down to the sea like a great wooden helmet. The first sight of it dancing on the waves was as enchanting to him as the sight of a young foal skipping in a meadow. He had made himself a double-ended paddle, being inhibited from attempting any kind of sail by the recollection of his over-ambitious efforts with the *Escape*. He made a series of excursions round the island which completed his knowledge of his domain but which made him realize, more than anything else he had done, the extent of his solitude.

Journal

Solitude is not a changeless state imposed on me by the wreck of the *Virginia*. It is a corrosive influence which acts on me slowly but ceaselessly, and in one sense purely destructively. On my first day here I was divided between two human societies, both imaginary – the vanished crew and the people of the island, which I supposed to be inhabited. I was still warm from contact with my fellow-men, continuing in my mind the dialogue cut short by the disaster. Then the island turned out to be deserted. I was in a land bereft of human kind. The group of my unfortunate companions receded into darkness, and their voices had long been silent when my own was still only beginning to weary of its soliloquy. Since then I have noted with a horrid fascination the dehumanizing process which I feel to be inexorably at work within me.

I know now that every man carries within himself – and as it were above himself – a fragile and complex framework of habits, responses, reflexes, preoccupations, dreams and associations, formed and constantly transformed by perpetual contact with his fellows. Deprived of its sap this delicate growth withers and dissolves. My fellow-men were the mainstay of my world . . . Each day I measure my debt to them by observing the fresh cracks in my personal structure. I know what I would suffer should I lose the use of words, and with all the power of my anguish I seek to combat that final surrender. But my relationship to material things is also undermined by solitude. When a painter or engraver introduces human figures into a landscape or alongside a monument, they are not there merely as an accessory. Human figures *convey the scale*, and what is still more important, they represent attitudes, possible points of view, which enrich the picture for the outside observer by providing him with other, indispensable points of reference.

But in Speranza there is only one viewpoint, my own, deprived of all context. And this shedding of context was not completed in a day. At first, and as it were instinctively, I projected possible observers – parameters – on to hilltops or behind rocks or into the branches of trees. The island was thus charted by a network of interpolations and extrapolations which lent it different aspects and rendered it meaningful. That is what every normal man does in a normal situation. I became aware of this function – with many others – only when I found it dying within me. Today the process is complete. My vision of the island is reduced to that of my own eyes, and what I do not see of it is to me a total unknown. Everywhere where I am not total darkness reigns. I find, indeed, as I write these lines that the experience I am seeking to define is not only without precedent but that it contradicts in their essence the very words I am using. Language in a fundamental manner evokes the *peopled* world, where other men are like so many lamps casting a glow of light around them within which everything is, if not known, at least knowable. Those lights have vanished from my consciousness. For a long time, fostered by imagination, they continued to reach me. Now it is over, and the darkness has closed in.

But my solitude does not only destroy the meaning of things. It undermines them at the very root of their being. More and more do I come to doubt the evidence of my senses. I know now that the very earth beneath my feet needs to be trodden by feet other than mine if I am to be sure of its substance. Optical illusions, mirages, hallucinations, waking dreams, imagined sounds, fantasy and delirium . . . against these aberrations the surest guard is our brother, our neighbour, our friend or our enemy – anyway, God save us, *someone*!

Yesterday, on my way through the small wood leading to the grasslands on the south-eastern coast, I was brought to a standstill by a smell which took me suddenly and almost painfully back to my father's house, to the office where he was in the habit of receiving customers; but on a Monday morning, the day when visitors were not admitted and when my mother, helped by one of the neighbours, polished the floor. The impression was so powerful, so incongruous, that once again I doubted my reason. For a moment I struggled against that memory, which was one of overpowering sweetness; then I let my thoughts slip back into the past, to that empty museum, that dead world, varnished like a coffin, which called to me with such seductive tenderness. Finally the illusion loosed its hold on me. Walking on through the wood I came upon some shrubs of terebinth, of which the bark, cracking in the heat, exuded an amber-coloured resin whose powerful odour had evoked all the Monday mornings of my childhood.

Because it was a Tuesday morning Robinson, in accordance with his work-schedule, was on a strip of beach newly uncovered by the tide, collecting a particular kind of clam with rather tough flesh but a pleasant flavour which he could keep for a week by storing them in a jar of sea-water. He wore a round hat of the kind used by British sailors, a pair of wooden clogs, breeches which left his calves bare and a

4

loose cotton shirt. The sun, to which his pale, red-head's skin was so sensitive, was veiled by a curtain of cloud lumpy as astrakhan, and he had been able to leave his parasol in the cave, although he seldom went anywhere without it. It was low water, and after crossing over beds of broken shells, strips of mud and shallow pools, he had come a sufficient distance from Speranza to be able to see the island's green, yellow and black mass as a whole. Having no one else to talk to he discoursed with her in a slow, deep dialogue in which his movements, his acts and undertakings, were so many questions to which she replied with the favour or disfavour that greeted them. He no longer doubted that everything must henceforth depend on his relations with Speranza and his success in ordering their joint affairs. He was always on the alert for the responses that came to him from her in a thousand forms, sometimes ciphered and sometimes symbolic.

He came to a flat, weed-covered rock surrounded by a pool of clear water, and he was amusedly watching the antics of a small, intrepid crab which was defying him with two upraised pincers of unequal size, like a hired assassin with sword and dagger, when he was struck dumb with amazement at seeing the imprint of a naked foot. It would not have surprised him to come upon his own traces in the sand or mud, although he had long since given up going without clogs, but this footprint was sunk into *the rock itself*. Was it that of some other man? Or had he been so long on the island that the imprint of his foot in the sandy slime covering the rock had had time to become petrified? He took off his right clog and set his foot in the imprint, which was half-filled with sea-water. That was precisely what it was. His foot fitted the imprint as though he were putting on a well-worn slipper. There could be no doubt about it, no fantasy or mystification; it was not Adam's footprint when he had taken possession of the Garden, or that of Venus rising from the sea; it was his personal signature, the unique token of Robinson, impressed in the living rock and thus made indelible and eternal. Like one of the free-ranging cattle herds on the Argentine pampas, which bear the mark of the branding-iron, Speranza bore the seal of her lord and master.

The maize-crop failed completely, and the plot of land where Robinson had sown it was reverting to its original, overgrown state. But the wheat and barley were both doing well, and Robinson experienced the first delight Speranza had given him – how sweet and deep it was! – when he caressed those tender, blue-tinted shoots. It took great strength of mind to refrain from pulling out the weeds that here and there disfigured his neatly ordered rows, but he could not infringe the Biblical injunction which lays down that the good grain must not be separated from the tares before the harvest. He consoled himself with the thought of the golden loaves he would soon be bringing out of the oven he had carved in the soft stone in a wall of the cave. A brief spell of rainy weather caused him to tremble for the slender stalks as they bowed under the burden of heavy heads weighted with water. But then the sun shone again and they stood upright, swaying in the breeze like an army of small horses curvetting with plumed headgear.

When the time came for harvesting Robinson decided, since he had no scythe or sickle, that the most appropriate of the few implements he possessed was the old boarding-cutlass he had retrieved from the *Virginia,* where it had hung in the Captain's cabin. His first thought had been to proceed in an orthodox fashion, using a stick to hold the stalks upright while the blade swept through them. But as he took that warlike weapon in his hand a strange frenzy seized him, and forgetting the rules he slashed about him in all directions, furiously shouting as he did so. Not many of the heads were damaged by this treatment, but he lost a good deal of the straw.

That harvest-day, which should have celebrated the first fruits of my labour and the fruitfulness of Speranza, was more like a desperate battle against nothing. How far I still am from the perfect life in which every action is governed by the laws of economy and harmony! I let myself be carried away like a child in an outburst of disorder, and I recaptured none of the light-hearted joys I had known when haymaking in the West Riding. The rhythmic movement, the swing of the arms from right to left, which the body balances by swaying from left to right, the scythe-blade cutting into the yielding, flowery mass and laying its swathe at my left hand, the heady scent of juice and sap – all this constituted a simple happiness in which I could delight without repining. The whetted blades were so supple that they could be seen to bend first one way and then the other. The meadow was a growing mass to be attacked and conquered, methodically laid low, step by step and line by line. But it was an intricately contrived mass, an array of minute living entities, a vegetable world in which matter was wholly subjected to form. That infinite variety of the European meadow is the exact opposite of the amorphous, undifferentiated herbage I cut down here. Nature in the tropics is powerful, but crude and simple as the glaring blue sky. Alas, when shall I again see our pale skies and the exquisite greys of the mist rising over the valley of the Ouse?

Having threshed his wheat and barley by flailing it in a sail folded in two, Robinson winnowed the grain by pouring it from one container into another on a windy day, letting the husks and chaff blow where they would. He enjoyed that work of purification, simple but not wearisome, for the spiritual symbols it evoked. His spirit rose up to God, beseeching Him to cause the frivolous thoughts that filled his mind to scatter in the winds, leaving behind only the solid seeds of wisdom. When the winnowing was done he found with pride that his harvest amounted to thirty gallons of wheat and twenty of barley. He had prepared a pestle and mortar to grind his flour – a hollowed tree-stump and a heavy branch knotted at one end – and the fire beneath the oven was laid in readiness for the first baking. And then, on a sudden impulse, he resolved to eat none of that first crop.

Journal

I had been keenly looking forward to the first loaf to come out of the soil of Speranza, out of my oven and the labour of my hands. But it must wait till later. Later . . . The wealth of promise in that simple word! What suddenly dawned upon me with an overwhelming certainty is my need to fight against time, that is to say, to imprison time. Insofar as I live from day to day, I let myself drift; time slips through my fingers, and in losing time I lose myself. Indeed, the whole problem of this island may be expressed in terms of time, and it is no accident if, at the lowest level, I started by living here as though I were outside time. When I began a calendar I regained possession of myself. But now I must do more. None of this first harvest of wheat and barley must be swallowed up by the present. It must be preserved as a source of strength for the future. I shall divide it into two parts, one part seed for the next sowing and the other a provision for contingencies, lest the promise of the second harvest be not kept.

Henceforth I shall abide by the following rule: all production is creation, therefore good; all consumption is destruction, therefore bad. My situation is in fact not unlike that of my fellow-countrymen who land by shiploads on the coasts of the New World. They too must bow to the law of accumulation. For them too the wasting of time is a crime and the saving of time a cardinal virtue. To accumulate! Once again I am reminded of the wretchedness of my solitude. Where I am concerned, to sow and reap is good: the evil sets in when I grind and knead and bake, for then I am working only for myself. The American colonist need have no misgivings about making bread; he will sell the bread, and the money he stores in his chest represents the saving of time and work. But I in my solitude am deprived of the benefits of money, although I have no lack of it.

Today I can measure the folly and malice of those who affect to despise money, that divine institution. Money spiritualizes all that it touches by endowing it with a quality that is both rational (measurable) and universal, since property reckoned in terms of money is accessible to all men. Venality is one of the cardinal virtues. The venal man suppresses his murderous and anti-social instincts – honour, self-pride, patriotism, political ambition, religious fanaticism, racialism – in favour of his need to co-operate with others, his love of fruitful exchanges, his sense of human solidarity. The term 'the Golden Age' should be taken literally, and I see now that mankind would swiftly achieve it were its affairs wholly in the hands of venal man. Alas, it is nearly always high-minded men who make history, and so the flames destroy everything and blood flows in torrents. The plump merchants of Venice afford us an example of the luxurious happiness possible in a State governed solely by the law of lucre, whereas the emaciated wolves of the Spanish Inquisition show us the infamies of which men are capable when they have lost the love of material well-being. The Huns would soon have checked their advance if they had known how to profit by the riches they had conquered. Encumbered with their gains, they would have stayed to enjoy them, and life would have resumed its course. But they were disinterested savages. They despised gold. They rushed onwards, burning as they went.

Thereafter Robinson entered on a course of frugal living while he laboured intensively to develop the resources of the island. He cleared and tilled whole acres of meadow and forest, sowed a field of turnips, sorrel and other vegetables that grew sporadically in the south, protected newly planted palm-trees against the depredations of birds and insects, set up a dozen skeps which were gradually occupied by wild bees, and near the water's edge dug ponds of salt and fresh water in which he bred bream and angel-fish and even sea-shrimps. He laid in huge stores of dried fruit, smoked meat, salt fish and small cheeses which were hard and gritty as chalk but kept indefinitely. And finally he discovered a method of producing a kind of sugar with which to make jam and preserve fruit. It was derived from a variety of palm, thicker in the middle than it was at the top or bottom, which exuded a great quantity of very sweet sap. Felling one of these trees he cut off its crown of foliage, and the sap immediately began to ooze out of its upper end. It continued to do this for some months, but he had to cut off a fresh slice every day, because the pores had a tendency to close. A single tree gave him ninety gallons of this molasses, which solidified into an enormous cake.

Journal

Tenn, my faithful shipmate, has returned to me. I find it impossible to express the happiness contained in those words. I shall never know where or how he has been living since the wreck, but at least I think I can understand what caused him to avoid me. He appeared while I was working like a madman on the *Escape*, only to beat an instant retreat, furiously growling. In my blindness I wondered whether the terror of the shipwreck, followed by a long period of solitude in hostile country had not caused him to revert to the savage state. Incredible complacency! It was I who was the savage, not he, and I cannot doubt that my wild expression and frenzied manner terrified the poor creature, who had remained more civilized than I. There is no lack of instances of dogs who have been compelled almost against their will to desert a master sunk in the depths of degradation or folly, and I know of none which would allow its master to eat out of the same bowl as itself. Tenn's return rejoices my heart because it testifies to my victory over the destructive forces which were dragging me towards the abyss. The dog is the natural companion of man, but not of the noisome and degenerate creature which misfortune, stripping him of human semblance, may make of him. Henceforth I shall read in Tenn's trusting eyes whether I am capable of preserving my stature of a man, despite the fate that threatens to destroy me.

But Robinson could not wholly regain his human dignity except by providing himself with a better dwelling than was afforded by a cave or a screen of leaves. Being now in company with the most domesticated of all animals, he needed to build himself a proper setting for domesticity, a domus, a house.

He resolved to situate it near the entrance to the cave where all his wealth was stored, which was also at the highest point of the island. To begin with, he dug a wide rectangular trench some three feet deep, which he filled with branches covered by a thick layer of white sand. On this drained foundation he set up walls of palm-logs, grooved to fit together, the interstices being filled by the scaly bark with its growth of vegetable matting. He constructed a double-sided roof of light poles plaited with reed which he covered with the leaves of rubber-plants, using them like slates. He plastered the outside of the walls with a mortar made of clay and chopped straw, and completed his sand floor with a rough paving of flat stones, over which he spread goatskins and straw mats. A few articles of furniture made of osier, the dishes and lanterns he had retrieved from the *Virginia*, the spyglass, the cutlass and one of the muskets hanging on the wall created an atmosphere of comfort and even intimacy in which he constantly rejoiced. Seen from outside, that first dwelling had a surprising look of a tropical peasant's cabin, crude but neat, fragile as to its roof but with massive walls, which seemed to Robinson to express the paradox of his own situation. He was conscious both of its practical inadequacy and of its symbolic, and above all moral, importance in his life. He soon resolved not to use it for any workday purpose, not even for cooking, and only to sleep in it on Saturday nights, continuing during the rest of the week to sleep on the litter of straw and feathers which he installed in the alcove he had dug in the rocky wall of the cave. By degrees the hut became for him a sort of shrine of human living, and he never entered it without the sense of accomplishing a ritual act. He even fell into the habit – having unpacked the garments contained in the chests brought from the

56

Virginia, some of which were very handsome – of only entering it in suitable attire, jacket, breeches, stockings and shoes, as though he were paying a formal call on what was best in himself.

He later realized that the sun was only visible from inside the building at certain hours of the day and that something was needed which would enable him to measure the passing of time. Accordingly, after a number of experiments, he contrived a primitive clepsydra, or water-clock, out of a glass demijohn in the bottom of which he pierced a very small hole through which the water escaped drop by drop into a brass bowl placed beneath it. By trial and error he found the precise amount of water needed for it to empty itself in twenty-four hours, and he then marked the hours in rings round the jar, numbering them with Roman numerals. This water-clock was an immense comfort to him. Listening by day and night to the regular 'plop' of water dropping into the bowl, he had a feeling that time was no longer slipping away in his despite; that he had regulated and mastered time – in a word, tamed it, just as the whole island was gradually to be tamed by the strength and resolution of a single man.

Journal

Henceforth whether I am waking or sleeping, writing or cooking a meal, my time is marked by this regular ticking, positive, un-answerable, measurable and precise. How eagerly I seek those adjectives which for me represent so many victories over the forces of evil! I demand, I insist, that everything around me shall hence-forth be measured, tested, certified, mathematical and rational. One of my tasks must be to make a full survey of the island, its distances and its contours, and incorporate all these details in an accurate surveyor's map. I should like every plant to be labelled, every bird to be ringed, every animal to be branded. I shall not be content until this opaque and impenetrable place, filled with secret ferments and malignant stirrings, has been transformed into a calculated design, visible and intelligible to its very depths!

But shall I have the strength to complete the formidable task? Do I possess in myself the massive dose of rationality I wish to administer to Speranza? The regular plop of the clepsydra, which a moment ago soothed me with its deliberate, consoling music, like the ticking of a metronome, now evokes in me an opposite and terrifying thought: that of the inexorable dripping of water which wears away a stone. I cannot dismiss it from my mind, and my whole philosophy trembles. The disintegration of language is the most evident sign of this process of erosion.

Although I constantly talk aloud, never letting an observation or an idea enter my head without proclaiming it to the trees or the clouds, I note with every day that passes the collapse of whole sectors of that citadel of words within which our thought dwells and moves, like a mole in its network of tunnels. Those fixed points which thought uses for its progression, like crossing a river on stepping-stones, are crumbling and vanishing beneath the surface. I am losing my sense of the meaning of words which do not represent concrete objects. I can only talk literally. Metaphor, litotes and hyperbole call for a considered effort which has the effect of emphasizing everything that is unreal and conventional in those figures of speech. I can imagine that this mental travail would be of extreme interest to a grammarian or philologist; but to me it is a luxury that is both useless and destructive. For example, the notion of *depth*, which I never troubled to scrutinize when using it in such expressions as 'a deep thinker' or 'a deep love'. It is a strange prejudice which sets a higher value on depth than on breadth, and which accepts 'superficial' as meaning, not 'of wide extent' but 'of little depth', whereas 'deep', on the other hand, signifies 'of great depth' and not 'of small surface'. Yet it seems to me that a feeling such as love is better measured, if it can be measured at all, by the extent of its surface than by its degree of depth. For I measure my love for a woman by the fact that I love indiscriminately her hands, her eyes, her carriage, the clothes she wears, the commonplace things she merely touches, the place where she dwells, the sea in which she bathes . . . All this, it seems to me, is decidedly on the surface! Whereas a lesser love aims directly – *in depth* – at sex, and leaves all the rest in a half-light of disregard.

A similar process of thought – which has recently begun to grate on me when I seek to apply it – prefers the inward to the outward being. Men are to be regarded as riches enclosed in a worthless shell, and the more deeply we penetrate within them, the greater is the treasure we discover. But what if there were no treasure? What if that outer shell were solid, filled with sameness like a doll stuffed with bran? I know only too well – I to whom no one comes to lend me a countenance or enrich me with secrets – that I am no more than an emptiness in the heart of Speranza, an attitude to Speranza – a viewpoint, a nothing. I think the soul only acquires any notable content from beyond that barrier of skin which separates the inner from the outer world, and that it enriches itself only inasmuch as it flows out in widening circles from that central point which is Me. Robinson can only be infinitely rich when he merges with Speranza as a whole.

On the following day Robinson laid the foundations of a *Conservatory of Weights and Measures.* He built it in the form of a pavilion, but constructed of the most intractable materials he could find, blocks of granite with bond-stones of laterite. In it he placed a sort of altar, as though it were an idol, and on the walls – like a panoply of the weapons of reason – he arrayed the measures of an inch, a foot, a yard, a rod, a cable's length, a pint, a peck, a bushel, a gallon, a grain, a dram, and an ounce and a pound avoirdupois.

Chapter 4

On Day 1000 by his calendar Robinson dressed himself in formal attire and closed the door of his official Residence. Standing at a desk which he had designed to enable him to write in an upright position, and in an attitude of solemn formality, he wrote in the largest of the sea-washed volumes he had brought off the *Virginia*:

CHARTER OF THE ISLAND OF SPERANZA INAUGURATED ON THE 1000th DAY OF THE LOCAL CALENDAR

ARTICLE THE FIRST. By virtue of the Inspiration of the Holy Spirit, interpreted and obeyed in conformity with the teachings of the Revered Friend, George Fox, Robinson Crusoe, born at York on 19 December 1737, is hereby appointed Governor of the Island of Speranza, situated in the Pacific Ocean between the islands of Juan Fernandez and the coast of Chile. As holder of this Office he has full Powers of Legislation and Execution throughout the Territory of the Island and its territorial waters, in accordance with the dictates of the Inner Light.

ARTICLE II. The inhabitants of the island are required to express aloud all such thoughts as may occur to them, in a clear and audible voice.

Gloss. The loss of the faculty of speech from lack of practice in its use is among the most humiliating disasters that threaten me. Already when I speak aloud I am conscious of a thickness of the tongue, as though after an excess of wine. It is important therefore that the inward discourse which we pursue in our minds during all our conscious moments should be spoken by my lips, that they may be constantly exercised. This is indeed a natural tendency, and it calls for perpetual vigilance lest the words be uttered before the thought is formulated, as happens with children and old people who babble aloud in the weakness of their wits.

ARTICLE III. It is forbidden to perform one's natural functions except in the places reserved for that purpose.

Gloss. That this ordinance should rank as Article III of the Charter may cause surprise. But the Governor must legislate in the light of necessity as it presents itself, and in view of the moral laxity that menaces the inhabitants of the island it is essential that some small discipline should be imposed on them in a sector of their life where they are on a level with the animals.

ARTICLE IV. Friday is a day of fasting.

ARTICLE V. Sunday is a day of rest. At seven o'clock on Saturday evening all work on the island will cease and the inhabitants will don their best attire for dinner. On Sunday morning at ten they will gather in the Meeting House to meditate on a text from the Holy Scriptures.

ARTICLE VI. The Governor alone is permitted to smoke tobacco. But he may do so only on Sunday afternoon during the current month, once a fortnight in the ensuing month, once only in the next month, and thereafter only once every other month.

Gloss. I have only recently discovered the pleasures afforded by the late Van Deyssel's china-bowled pipe. Alas, the tobacco in his jar will last only a very short time. I must prolong it as far as possible, and not fall into a habit of which the deprivation would later cause me discomfort.

At this point Robinson paused. Closing the Book of the

Charter, he opened another volume, equally unsullied, and wrote in capital letters on the title-page:

PENAL CODE OF THE ISLAND OF SPERANZA, INSTITUTED ON THE 1000th DAY OF THE LOCAL CALENDAR

He turned the page, and after careful reflection wrote:

ARTICLE THE FIRST. Failure to observe the Charter may be visited with two penalties: fasting and ditch-digging.

Gloss. These are the only penalties capable of being applied, since corporal punishment and the death penalty require an increase in the population. The ditch is situated in the stretch of meadowland between the outcroppings of rock and the first marshes. It is exposed to the full glare of the sun during the six hottest hours of the day.

ARTICLE II. All wallowing in the mire is strictly forbidden. Those contravening this order will be punished with a double stint of ditching.

Gloss. The ditch thus becomes the antithesis and in a sense the antidote to the mire. This Article subtly illustrates the principle whereby a wrongdoer shall be punished in the manner of his misdeed.

ARTICLE III. Whosoever pollutes the island with his excrement shall fast for one day.

Gloss. Another instance of the subtle relation between crime and punishment.

ARTICLE IV. . . .

Robinson made a further pause while he considered suitable penalties for offences against public morals within the confines of the island and its territorial waters. He went to the door and opened it, as though to show himself to his subjects. The rolling greenery of the tropical forest swept down to the sea, which further off merged with the sky,

Because he was red-headed as a fox his mother had clad him from childhood in green, teaching him to avoid blue, which, she said, did not suit the ginger of his hair and was inappropriate to his attire. But nothing could have been more harmonious at the moment than that sea of foliage against the background of sea and sky; and the whole scene, sun and sea, forest and empyrean, was fixed in a state so motionless that time itself might have seemed to be held in suspense had it not been for the liquid ticking of his clock. If, Robinson reflected, there is ever to be a Revelation, a manifestation of the Divine Spirit descending upon me, the legislator of Speranza, it should happen on a day and at a moment such as this. A tongue of flame dancing above my head, or a column of smoke rising like a spear to the zenith – would not these testify that I am the temple of God?

And as he uttered the words, speaking them aloud in accordance with Article II of the Charter, he saw beyond the curtain of the forest a thin wisp of smoke rising into the sky, apparently from the Bay of Salvation. Thinking at first that it was the answer to his prayer, he fell upon his knees uttering words of praise. But then a doubt entered his mind. Getting to his feet he went back into the Residence and equipped himself with his musket, a bag of powder, a pouch of bullets and the spyglass. He whistled to Tenn and plunged into the undergrowth, avoiding the direct path he had made from the cave to the foreshore.

About forty dark-skinned men were grouped in a circle round a fire from which a column of thick, milky smoke of unnatural density was now rising. Three long canoes with outriggers had been hauled up on to the beach. They were of the type common throughout the Pacific, remarkable for their seaworthiness despite their narrowness and shallow draught. As for the men, Robinson identified them through his glass as coastal Indians from the redoubtable tribe of the Araucanians, inhabiting the central part of Chile, who had held the Inca invaders at bay and inflicted bloody defeats on the Spanish *conquistadores*. They were short, sturdy men clad only in crude leather aprons. Their broad faces, with remarkably wide-separated eyes, were rendered stranger still by their custom of completely plucking their eyebrows, and by the thick, black, gleaming head of beautifully kept hair which they shook proudly on every pretext. Robinson had seen something of them during visits to Temuco, their capital in Chile, and he knew that if another war had broken out between them and the Spanish no white man could look for mercy at their hands.

That they had accomplished the long passage from the Chilean mainland was by no means impossible, considering the hardihood of their seafaring exploits, but is seemed more likely that they had come from one of the islands of the Juan Fernandez group, having settled there; and it was fortunate for Robinson that chance had not caused him to blunder into their midst, since he would probably have been killed at once, or at the best enslaved.

Knowing what he did of the customs of their country, he could guess the nature of the ceremony that was now taking place. An emaciated, wild-haired woman, dancing and quivering within the circle of men, drew near to the fire, flung a handful of powder into it, and ardently inhaled the dense white fumes that rose. Then, as though intoxicated, she turned towards the motionless circle and began to walk slowly round it, seeming to examine the men and pausing abruptly in front of one or two. She then returned to the fire and again inhaled the smoke, so that Robinson began to wonder whether, witch-doctor though she was, she would not fall asphyxiated before the ritual was complete. But no: the climax suddenly came. Rising to her full height in her shreds of garments, she stretched out her arms towards one of the men, while her wide-opened mouth seemed to cry maledictions that Robinson could not hear. The man thus singled out as responsible for whatever calamity had befallen them, sickness or drought, fell with his face to the ground, trembling violently. One of the others went up to him and with a *machete* cut away the wretched garment he was wearing. Then the *machete* descended in a series of regular blows, cutting off the head, arms and legs. The six sections of the body were cast on the flames, while the witch squatted on the sand as though in a trance.

The circle broke up and the men took no more interest in the fire, of which the smoke had turned black. They returned to their canoes, and six of them got out water-bags and disappeared under the trees. Robinson hastily drew back while still keeping a watchful eye on the invaders of his solitude. If they were to find any trace of his presence they might scour the island in search of him and he would be hard put to it to escape. Fortunately there was a fresh-water stream near by, and they had no need to penetrate inland. Carrying the filled water-bags slung from poles on their shoulders, the six men returned to the canoes, which the others had refloated. The witch was lying prostrate on a sort of throne erected in the stern of one of them.

When the three craft had vanished beyond the cliffs at the extremity of the bay Robinson went down to examine the funeral pyre. The charred remains of the victim were still visible. Thus, he reflected, do primitive peoples, unwittingly and with the cruelty that is natural to them, obey the behest of the *Gospel according to St Matthew*: '*Wherefore if thy hand or thy foot offend thee, cut them off and cast them from thee: it is better for thee to enter into life halt or maimed, rather than having two hands or feet to be cast into everlasting fire. And if thine eye offend thee, pluck it out . . .* ' But did not charity join with practical economy in counselling that it was better to dress the gangrened eye, better to purify the member of the community whose error had brought shame upon his fellows?

5

It was with a mind beset by doubts that the Governor of Speranza returned to his Residence.

ARTICLE VII. The Island of Speranza is declared a Fortified Place under the command of the Governor, who is hereby accredited with the rank of General. Curfew is obligatory one hour after sunset.

ARTICLE VIII. Sunday ceremonial is extended to include working days.

Gloss. Every increase in the pressure of events must be compensated by an equivalent increase in the strictness of behaviour. This calls for no elucidation.

Setting down his vulture's quill, Robinson looked about him. In front of the Official Residence, the Pavilion of Weights and Measures, the Palace of Justice and the Meeting House there was now a crenellated curtain-wall made from the excavation of a dry-moat twelve feet deep and ten feet wide running in an ample semi-circle from one side of the cave to the other. The two flint-lock muskets and the double-barrelled pistol were ready in position in its three central loopholes: in case of an attack Robinson could delude his assailants into believing that he was not the only defender. The boarding cutlass and the axe were also in readiness, although it was unlikely that it would ever come to hand-to-hand fighting because the approaches to the battlements were thickly sown with snares. First came a number of pits in staggered rows, concealed by tufts of grass or reed matting, each with a sharp wooden spike in the centre. In the clearing at the entrance to the footpath leading to the bay, at the point where an enemy force might pause to regroup before making its final advance, Robinson had buried a barrel of gunpowder with a fuse of tow so that it could be exploded at a distance. And finally the bridge over the moat was, of course, capable of being raised from within.

The work of fortification, and his constant fear lest the

Araucanians should return, had kept Robinson in a state of suspense which was both morally and physically bracing. Once again he found that to build, to organize and to make and abide by rules were sovereign remedies against the demoralizing effects of solitude. Never had he felt so far removed from the temptation of the mire. Every evening before curfew he went on his round accompanied by Tenn, who seemed to understand the danger that threatened them. The fortress was then 'locked up' for the night. Small boulders were rolled into positions calculated to cause possible assailants to fall into the pits. The drawbridge was raised, all entrances were barricaded, and the curfew was rung. Robinson then prepared his evening meal, laid the table in the Residence and withdrew into his cave, to emerge a few minutes later washed and scented and clad in his coat of ceremony, with his hair combed and his beard trimmed. Finally, by the light of a candelabrum holding a bunch of twigs steeped in resin, he ate his dinner slowly under the watchful and worshipping eyes of Tenn.

This period of intense warlike activity was followed by a brief spell of heavy rain which entailed arduous labours of repair and maintenance, and then it was time for the wheat and barley harvest. The yield was so heavy that for additional storage room Robinson resorted to a small cave leading out of the main one, its entrance so narrow that hitherto he had made no use of it. And now he did not deny himself the pleasure of bread-making. He put aside a small part of his yield, and at last he was able to heat the oven which for so long he had kept in readiness. It was a tremendous event whose solemnity was by no means lost on him, although not until later did he appreciate its full importance. Once again he was sharing in that most material and at the same time most spiritual of human activities. But if that first baking in its mystical and universal significance took him to the very roots of mankind, it also harboured in

67

its twofold nature implications that were peculiar to himself – hidden, intimate, buried amid the shameful secrets of his early childhood – which foreshadowed an unforeseen flowering of his solitary state.

Journal

Kneading my dough for the first time this morning, I was visited by memories, long-buried under the business of living, which my isolation has revived. I was about ten when my father asked me what I wanted to be when I grew up. I replied unhesitatingly, a baker. He looked gravely at me and then nodded with a smile of affectionate approval. There can be no doubt that the humble calling was endowed with a particular dignity in his eyes, hallowed by the symbolism attaching to bread, the first food of the body and also the food of the soul, according to the sacramental tradition which his Quaker upbringing had taught him to reject while he held it in respect for its ancient origin.

For me there was something else, although at that time I had no thought of defining the especial fascination which the baker's trade held for me. On my way to school in the morning I passed a grating in a wall from which flowed a current of air, warm, maternal, as it were carnal, which had caused me to pause for a long time peering through the bars the first time I became aware of it. Surrounding me was the damp gloom of the early morning, the muddy street with the unhappy prospect of school and stern masters at its end. But in that lighted cellar I could see a baker's apprentice, stripped to the waist and covered with flour, plunging his arms to the elbow in a thick, creamy mass of dough. I have always preferred the feel of things to their look. The senses of touch and smell are to me more moving and instructive than those of sight and hearing. I do not think this speaks highly for my spiritual nature, but I humbly confess it. For me colour is but a promise of hardness or softness, and shape the token of a suppleness or rigidity that I can explore with my hands. I could conceive of nothing more pliable or yielding than that headless body of warm and sensuous matter submitting to the plunging caresses of a half-naked man. I know it now, there lurked in my mind the thought of a strange marriage between the dough and the baker, and I even dreamed of a new kind of yeast which would give the bread a musky savour, like a breath of spring.

Thus for Robinson the strenuous ordering of his island was accompanied by the growth, timid in the first instance, of tendencies of which he was still scarcely aware. It was indeed as though the framework, fragile but feverishly strengthened, which he was building around himself existed only to protect the evolution of a new man destined eventually to emerge. But Robinson did not yet know this, and he continued to despair at the imperfections of the structure he was creating. Indeed, his observance of the Charter and the Penal Code, the punishments he inflicted on himself, his rigid adherence to a time schedule that left him not a moment's respite, the ceremonial which accompanied all his major actions – this straitjacket of conventions and pre-scriptions which he resolutely wore in order to stay upright, did not prevent him from being agonizingly conscious of the wild and untamed presence of the tropical world surround-ing him, or, within himself, of the steady work of erosion effected by solitude on the soul of a civilized man. Although he might deny himself certain sentiments and certain in-stinctive inferences, he was constantly assailed by super-stitions and perplexities which threatened the stability of the edifice devised for his protection.

Thus he could not prevent himself from attributing a fateful significance to the call of a particular bird of which he did not know the name. This bird, always hidden in the trees, invisible but often very close to him, was given to uttering two distinct cries, one of which told unmistakably of happiness while the other sounded a terrifying note of ap-proaching danger. Robinson had come to be in mortal fear of that second call, yet he could not restrain himself from adventuring into the dank, sombre regions where the birds seemed to lurk, trembling in advance at their warning of harm.

He was becoming increasingly mistrustful of the evidence of his senses, inclined to dismiss things he thought he had seen or heard because of doubts of which he could not rid himself. And on the other hand he ceaselessly returned to the investigation of things which seemed to him improbable or suspect or contradictory. For example, while paddling in his canoe off the south-western coast of the island he was struck by the huge clamour of bird-calls and insect striations which came to him over the water as though borne on a series of waves. He went ashore; but as he penetrated beneath the trees he found himself enclosed in a silence that filled him with uneasy astonishment. Did it mean that this stirring of wild life was only to be heard from outside and at a distance, or was it he who had provoked the silence? He got back into the canoe and paddled away. But then he returned to the place and again went ashore, repeating the experiment several times, in weariness and exasperation, but unable to find an answer to the riddle.

And there were the dunes of coarse sand in the north-eastern corner from which came a sort of abysmal lowing sound, like the groaning of the earth itself, which froze him with horror, if only because of the impossibility of determining its cause. It was true that he seemed to have heard of a hill in Chile called *El Bramador* (a word which meant the belling of a stag) because when anyone walked on it the shifting of the sand set up a subterranean rumble. But had he really heard that tale or had he unconsciously invented it, simply to calm his fears? He could not be sure, and with a maniacal obstinacy he strode over those dunes keeping his mouth wide open, after the ancient belief of sailors, so that he might hear the better.

It is three o'clock in the morning, and I am wide awake. I wander along the damp passages of the cave. As a child I should have died of terror at the sight of those shadowy walls, the vaulted roofs vanishing into darkness, and at the sound of a drop of water falling on a stone. Solitude is strong wine. Intolerable to a child, it offers a harsh intoxication to the man who has learned how to still the fluttering of his heart. May it not be that Speranza is the fulfilment of a destiny prescribed for me in my earliest years? We got to know each other, Solitude and I, during my long, contemplative walks on the banks of the Ouse, and when I shut myself away in my father's library with a supply of candles to last me through the night, and again in London when I refused to make use of letters of introduction to friends of our family. When the *Virginia* ended her career on the reefs of Speranza I entered solitude as naturally as one may enter religion after a too devout childhood. Solitude had awaited me on these shores from the beginning of time, with its enforced companion, silence . . .

Since I have been here I have become something of a specialist in silence, or in silences, as I should say. With my whole being intent like a single ear I note the particular quality of the silence at a given moment. There are airy, scented silences like a June night in England, others with the glaucous thickness of the mire, and yet others that are hard and sonorous as ebony. I find myself plumbing the tomb-like depths of night-silence in the cave with a vague, queasy pleasure that somewhat perturbs me. Even by day I have nothing to connect me with life – wife, children, friends, enemies, servants, customers – those anchors that keep our feet on earth. Why is it that in the heart of darkness I let myself stray so far, so deeply into the night? It may well be that presently I shall vanish without trace, sucked into the nothingness I shall have created around me.

The store of grain accumulating from year to year gave rise to serious problems because of the necessity to protect it against rats. The number of rats seemed to increase in exact proportion to the increasing supply of food, and Robinson constantly marvelled at this power of the animal world to adapt itself to the resources of its environment, unlike the human species, which multiplies the more when its wealth is less. But since he was resolved to continue amassing harvest after harvest while strength remained to him, he had to take drastic measures against parasites.

There were certain red-headed fungi that seemed to be poisonous since several young goats had died after eating them where they grew in the grass. Robinson made a decoction of these in which he soaked grains of wheat. He scattered the wheat along the paths followed by the rats, and they ate them and were none the worse. Then he devised cages with one-way doors; but he would have needed thousands of such traps to serve his purpose, and moreover the sight of those small, intelligent eyes glaring at him in hatred as he sank the cages in the river filled him with abhorrence. Solitude had rendered him intensely susceptible to anything resembling hostility to himself, even on the part of the most worthless of vermin. The carapace of indifference and mutual ignorance with which men shield themselves in their relations with one another had slipped from him, like a callous vanishing from an idle hand.

One day he witnessed a mortal combat between two rats. Blind and deaf to everything around them, they rolled over on the ground uttering furious squeaks until in the end each had ripped the throat out of the other and they died still locked in an embrace. Upon examining the bodies, Robinson found that they belonged to two quite different species. One was black, round and smooth-skinned, in every way similar to rats he had killed in the ships he had sailed in. The other was grey, longer in the body and with a thicker coat, a country rat such as he had seen in those parts of the grassland where they apparently lived. There could be no doubt that these were native to the island, whereas the first variety must be the descendants of the survivors from the

Virginia, now waxing plentiful on the fruits of his harvest. Both varieties appeared to have their own food supplies and their separate domains. Robinson confirmed this one evening by releasing in the grassland a black rat which he had captured in the cave. For a time only the quivering of the grass revealed the progress of an invisible hunt in which numerous small creatures were involved. Then the hunt narrowed, and a cloud of dust arose at the foot of one of the dunes. When Robinson reached the spot he found nothing left of his captive except its skin and bones. Accordingly he made a heap of two sacks of grain in that part of the meadow, and laid a trail from it to the cave. It was a heavy sacrifice that might have been wasted, but was not. That night the black rats came out in force to retrieve what they doubtless held to be their own property. A battle followed, and it was as though a storm had broken out over several acres of the meadow, raising countless small clouds of dust. The warring rats rolled over and over like living balls, while a sound of squealing filled the air as though from some infernal playground. Under the light of a brilliant moon the plain seemed to be boiling in a tumult of infant cries.

The outcome was what might have been expected. The animal which fights on enemy territory is always the loser. That night all the black rats perished.

Journal

Last night my right arm, which was hanging down from my couch, went to sleep, or 'died'. I took it in my left hand and lifted it up, that lifeless, heavy object of flesh and bone that might have been a part of some other person, attached to me in error. I dream of thus handling my whole body, marvelling at the dead weight, lost in the paradox of this *thing* which is myself. But is it really me? I remember my feeling as a child when, being taken into a church in York, I saw a stained-glass window depicting the martyrdom of St Denis. The saint had been decapitated on the steps of a shrine, and the headless body bent down and picked up the head in its two big hands . . . What caused me to marvel was not merely this evidence of prodigious vitality. To me in my infant piety the divine miracle was a commonplace, and besides, I had myself seen a duck running with its head cut off. No, the true marvel was that, being deprived of his head, St Denis had sought for it in the stream into which it had rolled, and that he had picked it up so carefully, with such affectionate solicitude. If it were I who had been beheaded I would certainly not have gone running after that unsightly object whose red hair and freckles were the bane of my life! How bitterly I deplored them, my flaming head of hair, long, skinny arms, legs like stilts and white body like that of a plucked goose with here and there a fluff of pinkish down. My hearty dislike of all this gave me a view of myself which has only achieved its fullness on Speranza. For some time indeed I have been performing an act of surgery on myself which consists of stripping away in turn all my attributes – I say *all* – like peeling an onion. And at the same time, I am constructing, separate from myself, a man called Crusoe, christian name Robinson, six feet tall, etc. . . . and I watch him live and grow on this island, without participating in his good fortune or suffering from his ill-chance. What 'I' is this? The question is far from an idle one, nor is it even unanswerable. Because if it is not *him* then it must be *Speranza*. There is a fluttering 'I' which comes to rest now on the man and now on the island, making of me one and the other by turns.

Is this not what is called 'philosophy', this that I have just written? What strange transformation is taking place within me that I, the most positive and least speculative of men, should be not only putting such questions to myself but, as it would seem, answering them! I must return to this matter.

His dislike of his own face, and an upbringing opposed to all personal vanity, had caused Robinson to keep away from the mirror he had brought from the *Virginia,* which he had hung on the least accessible part of the outside wall of the Residence. But his interest in this change he was undergoing drew him to it one morning, and he even brought out his chair so that he might more closely examine the only human face it was given to him to observe.

Although there was no marked alteration in his features he scarcely recognized himself. A single word occurred to him – disfigured. 'I am disfigured,' he said aloud, while despair clutched his heart. Vainly did he search, in the tightness of the mouth, the lacklustre eyes, the characterlessness of the forehead – faults with which he had always been familiar – for something to account for the shadowy distortion of the mask that gazed back at him through the dampstains in the mirror. The cause lay in something wider and deeper, a kind of hardness, a hint of death such as he had once seen in the face of a prisoner set free after years of captivity in a lightless dungeon. It was as though a winter of pitiless severity had passed over that familiar countenance, ridding it of all light and shade, petrifying its human tremors, simplifying its expression to the point of coarseness. Indeed, the square beard which framed it from one ear to the other had none of the flowing softness of the beard of the man from Nazareth! It belonged rather to the Old Testament with its summary justice, as did that over-direct gaze, alarming in its Mosaic harshness.

Like a new kind of Narcissus, plunged in distress and filled with a renewed self-distaste, Robinson spent a long time communing with his reflected self. He realized that the face is the part of our flesh which is endlessly moulded and remoulded, warmed by the presence of our fellows. After parting from someone with whom he has had an animated conversation, a man's face retains a glow which only gradually fades and may be rekindled if he meets someone else. 'An expressionless face. A degree of extinction such as perhaps no human being has ever before undergone.' Robinson spoke these words, too, aloud, but his face as he did so betrayed no more emotion than if his voice had issued from an instrument of brass. In an attempt at gaiety he sought to smile, but could not. There was in truth something frozen in his face, and it would have needed a long and happy reunion with his own kind to cause it to thaw. Only the smile of a friend could have given him back his smile.

Tearing himself away from the horrid fascination of the mirror, he gazed about him. Did he not possess everything he needed on this island? He could quench his thirst and appease his hunger, provide for his safety and even for his comfort, and the Bible was there to satisfy his spiritual needs. But who, by the simple power of a smile, would ever melt the ice that froze his countenance? He looked down at Tenn who was seated on the ground at his side gazing up at him. Was he dreaming? *Tenn was smiling at his master.* The black, finely serrated lip was curled back on one side of his mouth, disclosing a double row of fangs, while his head was comically inclined to one side and his nut-brown eyes seemed to be wrinkled in laughter. Robinson took the shaggy head between his hands while his own eyes grew misty with tenderness. A forgotten warmth tinged his cheeks, and he felt an unfamiliar tremor at the corners of his mouth – as when, on the banks of the Ouse, the first breath of March had heralded the approaching spring. Tenn was still smiling, and Robinson peered intently at him, seeking to recover that sweetest of human faculties. Thereafter it was like a game between them. Robinson would abruptly stop whatever he was doing – or even light a torch in the middle of the night – and, with a face now only half-dead, gaze at Tenn in a particular fashion. And Tenn would smile at him with his head on one side, and his dog's smile would be reflected ever more clearly on the face of the man, his master.

There was a glow of pink in the dawn sky, but the grand concert of birds and insects had not yet begun. Not a breath of wind stirred the palms decorating either side of the open door of the Residence. Robinson had awakened much later than usual. He realized this at once, but, no doubt because his conscience was still asleep, he did not rebuke himself. He lay picturing in his mind the day that awaited him beyond the door. First his toilet, then the reading of a passage of the Bible at the lectern, then the saluting of the colours and the formal opening of his citadel. He would let down the drawbridge and shift the boulders blocking the way to it. His morning would be devoted to his livestock. The nanny-goats numbered B13, L24, G2 and Z17 must be taken to be served by males. With a certain disgust Robinson pictured their indecent haste as he led them, skinny legs quivering and dugs flapping, to the male enclosure. He would leave them there all the morning to fornicate as they pleased. Then he must visit the artificial rabbit-warren he was seeking to establish. It was a sandy, hollow, overgrown with gorse and broom, around which he had built a low drystone wall, tilling within it small crops of turnips, lucerne and oats, in the hope of persuading a colony of agoutis to settle there – a variety of short-eared golden hare, of which he had been able to kill very few since he had been on Speranza. Also, he must find time before lunch to raise the water-level in his three freshwater fishponds, which were beginning to feel the drought. After this he would have a snack and then change into his general's uniform, because that afternoon he had to perform a series of official functions: he had to announce the result of the census of sea-turtles, take the chair at the Drafting Committee of the Charter and Penal Code, and finally preside at the opening of a new bridge of lianas flung audaciously across a ravine a hundred feet deep in the heart of the forest.

He lay wondering whether in addition to all this he would find time to complete the summer-house of tree-fern he had begun to build at the edge of the forest overlooking the bay, which was to serve not only as a look-out post commanding an excellent view of the sea, but also as a cool retreat in the heat of the day: and suddenly he realized why it was that he had awakened so late. He had forgotten to fill his water-clock the night before, and it had run dry. Indeed, it was the falling of the last drop into the copper bowl that drew his attention to the unaccustomed silence. Turning to look at it, he saw that the drop that should have followed was clinging uncertainly to the bottom of the glass jar; it stretched till it was pear-shaped, hesitated, and then, as though discouraged, resumed its spherical shape; and finally it returned whence it had come, not merely refusing to fall but seeming to reverse the passage of time.

Robinson stretched luxuriously on his couch. This was the first occasion for months when the inexorable dripping had not dictated his every movement as rigorously as if it had been a conductor's baton. Time had had a stop, and he was on holiday! He sat on the edge of the couch, and Tenn came and laid his muzzle on his knee. So it seemed that Robinson's omnipotence over this island, born of his solitude, extended even to the mastery of time. He reflected with delight that he had only to plug the hole in the water-clock and he could suspend the passing of the hours whenever he chose.

He got up and stood in the doorway, and such was his state of happy astonishment that he found that he was trembling and had to lean his shoulder against the doorpost. Later, reflecting on that wave of ecstasy and seeking to put a name to it, he called it a 'moment of innocence'. He had thought at first that the stopping of the clock had done no more than interfere with the routine of his day and make it appear less urgent; but now he perceived that the pause was less his affair than that of the island as a whole. It was as though in ceasing to reach out to each other according to their habit – and to their exhaustion – things had returned each to the essence of itself, were flowering in their own right and existing simply for their own sakes, seeking no other warrant than their own fulfilment. A great tenderness filled the heavens as though God, in a sudden outpouring of love, were resolved to bless all His creation. There was a radiance in the air; and in a moment of inexpressible happiness Robinson seemed to discern *another island* behind the one where he had so long dwelt in solitude, a place more living, warmer and more fraternal, that had been concealed from him by the prosaicness of his daily preoccupations.

This was a wonderful discovery. It seemed after all that it was possible to escape from the relentless discipline of the work-schedule and the ceremonial, without of necessity returning to the mire. Change was possible without decay! He could break the equilibrium so laboriously acquired and raise himself yet higher, instead of falling back. Unquestionably he had advanced another step in the transformation that was at work in the most hidden depths of himself. But all this was no more than a flash of revelation. In a moment of ecstasy the grub had seen that one day it would fly. Intoxicating, but a momentary vision, nothing more.

Thereafter he frequently stopped the clock, to pursue experiments which one day, perhaps, would cause the new Robinson to emerge from the chrysalis wherein he still slumbered. But the time was not yet. The *other island* did not show itself again in the rosy mist of dawn, as it had done on that memorable morning. Patiently he resumed his customary garments and went on with the game where he had left off, forgetting in the routine of small tasks and ceremonies that for a moment he had dreamed of other things.

Journal

I am not versed in philosophy, but the long periods of meditation to which I am inescapably reduced, and above all the crumbling, as it were, of certain of my mental faculties owing to my lack of human society, have led me to certain conclusions regarding the ancient riddle of consciousness. It seems to me, in a word, that the presence of others – and their unregarded intrusion into all our thinking – is a serious cause of confusion and obscurity in the relationship between the knower and the known. This does not mean that others have not an essential part to play in that relationship, but that it should take place at the proper time and in the light of day, not at inappropriate moments and as it were by stealth.

A candle carried in a darkened room throws its light on particular objects while leaving the rest in darkness. Things emerge for a moment into light and then return to shadow. But whether or not the light has caught them they do not change, either in their nature or in the fact of their existence. Such as they were before the light fell upon them, such are they during and after its passing.

This is our customary image, more or less, of the act of knowledge, the candle representing the knower and the lighted object the known. But what solitude has taught me is this: that this precept is concerned with the knowledge of things by *others*, that is to say, with a particular and narrow aspect of the problem of knowledge. A stranger entering any house who notices certain things, then turns to look at others – this corresponds precisely to the image of the candle moving through a darkened room. But the problem of knowledge as a whole must be defined at an earlier and more fundamental stage: for if I am to talk of a stranger entering my house and noting the things he finds there, I must myself be there, seeing the room and observing the conduct of the stranger.

Thus there are two problems of knowledge, or rather two kinds of knowledge, between which a sharp distinction must be made, but which I should doubtless have gone on confusing had not my present fate induced in me an entirely new view of things: there is knowledge *through others* and knowledge *through oneself*. To confound the two on the assumption that 'the other' is *another self*, is to get nowhere. Yet this is what we do when we depict the knower as any individual entering a room and seeing, touching, smelling – in a word, knowing – the objects he finds there. That individual is 'the other', but the things he sees are known to *me*, the observer of the scene. If therefore the problem is to be correctly stated I must depict the situation, not of another person entering the room, but of myself, speaking and seeing. Which I will now attempt to do.

A first point that must be noted, in attempting to depict the *self* unrelated to others, is that it exists only intermittently and, when all is said, comparatively seldom. Its presence corresponds to a secondary and as it were reflexive mode of knowledge. What happens in the primary, direct mode? Well, the objects are all there, shining in the sun or buried in the shade, rough or smooth, light or heavy; they are known, tested, touched, even cooked, carved, folded and so on; whereas I who do the knowing, the tasting, touching and cooking, have no separate existence except when I perform the act of reflection which causes *me* to emerge – a thing which in fact rarely happens. In that primary state of knowledge my awareness of an object is the object itself, the thing known and perceived without any person knowing and perceiving it. We cannot use the image of the candle shedding its light upon objects. We must substitute another: that of objects shining unaided, with a light of their own.

In that innocent, primary – as it were, primeval – stage which is our normal mode of existence there is a happy solitude of the known, a virginity of things comprising all things in themselves like so many functions of their own essence – colour, smell, taste, and form. In this sense Robinson *is* Speranza. He is conscious of himself only in the stir of myrtle leaves with the sun's rays breaking through, he knows himself only in the white crest of a wave running up the yellow sand.

Then suddenly there is a click. The subject breaks away from the object, divesting it of a part of its colour and substance. There is a rift in the scheme of things, and a whole range of objects crumbles in becoming *me*, each object transferring its quality to an appropriate subject. The light becomes the eye and as such no longer exists: it is simply the stimulation of the retina. The smell becomes the nostril – and the world declares itself odourless. The song of the wind in the trees is disavowed: it was nothing but a quivering of the tympani. Until finally the whole world has been absorbed into my soul which is the soul of Speranza, plucked out of the island, which then dies beneath my sceptical gaze.

An upheaval has taken place. Object has been roughly degraded to subject. No doubt it deserved to be, since this whole mechanism has a purpose. A knot of contradiction, a centre of discord, it has been eliminated from the body of the island, rejected, repudiated. The click represents a process which is the rationalization of the world. The world seeks its own reason and in doing so casts off that irrelevance, the subject.

One day a Spanish galleon came sailing towards Speranza. Nothing could have seemed more real. But it is more than a century since the last galleon vanished from the seas. And a feast was being held on board. But instead of anchoring and lowering a boat, the ship sailed past as though the shore were a thousand miles away. And a girl in old-fashioned clothes looked at me from a cabin window, and she was my sister, dead two decades ago. So many implausibilities were not acceptable. The click happened, and the galleon was stripped of its pretension to exist. It became Robinson's hallucination, absorbed into the subject, a haggard Robinson suffering from brain fever.

One day, while walking in the forest I saw a tree-stump in my path, fifty yards away. A strange tree-stump, hairy one would have said, looking something like an animal. And the stump moved. But this was impossible – tree-stumps do not move! And then it turned into a goat. But how could a tree-stump turn into a goat? The click was necessary, and it occurred. The stump vanished, not only in the present but in the past. There had never been a stump but only a goat. The stump was an illusion born of Robinson's defective eyesight.

The subject is the disqualified object. My eye is the corpse of light and colour. My nose is all that remains of odours when their unreality has been demonstrated. My hand refutes the thing it holds. Thus the problem of awareness is born of anachronism. It implies the simultaneous existence of the subject with the object, whose mysterious relationship to himself he seeks to define. But subject and object cannot exist apart from one another since they are one and the same thing, at first integrated into the real world and then cast out by it. Robinson is the excrement of Speranza.

This prickly formula gives me a sombre satisfaction. It shows me the rough and narrow road to salvation, at least to a kind of salvation – that of a fruitful and harmonious island, flawlessly cultivated and administered, strong in the harmony of all its attributes, steadily pursuing its course without me, because it is so close to me that even to look at it is to make it too much myself, so that I must shrink to become that intimate phosphorescence which causes each thing to be known while no one is the knower, each to be aware while no one has awareness . . . Oh, subtle and pure equilibrium, so fragile and so precious!

But Robinson was impatient to dismiss these dreams and speculations and tread the firm soil of Speranza. A day dawned when he believed he had found a positive road to the most intimate secrecy of the island.

Chapter 5

Situated at the centre of the island near the giant cedar-tree, like a giant air-vent at the base of the mass of rock, the cavern had always been of fundamental importance to Robinson, although for a long time he had used it only as a storehouse for his hoarded wealth: the growing stocks of grain, preserved fruit and salted meat; the tools and weapons, the chests of clothes and box of gold; finally, right at the back, the barrels of black powder which would have sufficed to blow up the whole island. Although he had long ceased to use firearms for hunting, Robinson attached great value to that stored destructive force, capable of being released whenever he chose, and to the sense of mastery it gave him. Armed like Jove with thunderbolts, he asserted his power of life and death over the island and its inhabitants.

But now the cave had come to assume a new significance for him. In his new life – the life which began when, putting aside his functions as governor, military commander and administrator, he stopped the waterclock – Speranza was no longer a territory to be exploited but a being, unquestionably feminine, towards whom were directed not only his philosophical speculations but also the new needs arising in his heart and flesh. He began to wonder confusedly whether the cave might not be the mouth or eye or some other orifice of that great body, and whether in exploring its whole extent he might not discover some hidden recess corresponding to the questions which were now stirring in his mind.

Beyond the powder-magazine was a narrow tunnel inclining steeply downwards which he had never explored until he entered what he was later to call the earthbound phase of his life. One reason was that the enterprise raised a problem of particular difficulty, that of lighting.

To adventure into those depths carrying a torch of resinous twigs, and he had nothing else, was to incur a serious risk from the proximity of the powder-barrels, of which he could not be sure that some part of the contents had not been spilt on the ground. It meant also that the motionless, rarefied air of the cave would be filled with dense, unbreathable fumes. After considering and dismissing the idea of driving a light-and-ventilation shaft from the surface to the far end of the cave, he found that he had no alternative but to accept the fact of darkness, to adapt himself to the exigencies of the new realm he sought to conquer; a thought which would certainly not have occurred to him a few weeks previously. But being now aware of the transformation he was undergoing, he was prepared to subject himself to the most vigorous discipline for the sake of what might turn out to be a new way of life.

He first made tentative efforts to accustom himself to darkness by feeling his way about the remoter parts of the cave. But he realized that this was not enough, and that a more drastic course of preparation was needed. He must go beyond the state of light-or-dark in which man normally lives, into the true world of the blind, which is complete and flawless, certainly less convenient to live in than the world of sight, and yet not wholly divorced from light or plunged in unrelieved darkness, as those with eyes suppose. The eye which invented light also invented darkness; those without eyes are ignorant of both, but they do not suffer from the absence of the former. The only way of attaining this state was to spend a very long time in total darkness, and this was what Robinson did, surrounded by wheat-cakes and jugs of goat's milk.

Around him absolute quiet prevailed. Not a sound penetrated the depths of the cave. Yet he already knew that the experiment was destined to succeed because he found that he was in no way cut off from Speranza. On the contrary, he lived intensely with her. Seated with his back to the rocky wall, his eyes wide-open in the darkness, he saw the white unfolding of the sea on all the shores of the island, the benevolent sway of palm-leaves stirred by the wind, the red flash of a humming-bird against a green sky. He smelt the moist freshness of the sand uncovered by the ebb, and watched a hermit-crab as it took the air at the doorway of its shell. A black-headed gull slowed suddenly in its flight to swoop down upon a small creature half-hidden in red seaweed gleaming brown in the drag of the undertow. Robinson's sense of solitude was dispelled in a strange fashion, not sidelong by winks and nudges, as when one is with a friend in a crowd, but centrally, as it were from the nucleus itself. He felt that he was near the core of Speranza, the beating heart, the mind whence ran the nerve-ends to all the parts of that great body, and into which flowed all intelligence coming from the surface: just as in some cathedrals there is a central point where by the play of sound-waves and vibrations one can hear the least sound, whether it comes from apse, choir, transept or nave.

The sun must be sinking towards the horizon. At the foot of the rocky pile which crowned the island the cave opened its black mouth like a round, astonished eye gazing over the sea. In a little while the sun would come level with it. Would the end of the cave be lighted by its rays? And for how long? Robinson was soon to learn, and, without being able to account for it, he attached great importance to the discovery.

The event when it happened was so quickly over that he wondered if it had been an optical illusion, a phosphorescent gleam in his own eyes, or even a lightning flash which had pierced the darkness without harming him. He had expected something like the raising of a curtain, a triumphant dawn, but it had been no more than a pinpoint of light in the black intensity that encompassed him. The tunnel must be either longer or less straight than he had thought. But what did this matter? The two eyes had met, the gaze of light and the gaze of darkness. A solar arrow had pierced the earthly soul of Speranza.

The next day the same thing happened. Time passed. The darkness persisted, although it had quite ceased to afflict him with the slight vertigo which causes the walker deprived of visible points of guidance to stumble. He was in the belly of Speranza like a fish in water, but he had still not attained that point beyond light and darkness which he felt to be the threshold of an absolute Beyond. Perhaps he should undertake a course of purification by fasting? In any case he had only a little milk left. He stayed where he was for another twenty-four hours, then got to his feet and, without hesitation or fear, but filled with a profound sense of the solemnity of the occasion, started towards the end of the tunnel. He had not gone far before he found what he was seeking, the mouth of a narrow vertical chimney. He made several unsuccessful attempts to slide down it. Although the walls were smooth as human flesh the opening was so small that his hips would not pass. Accordingly he stripped, and after rubbing his body with the remains of the milk, went headfirst into the bottleneck, and this time slid down slowly but steadily like food down a human gullet. After a very gentle descent which might have lasted for seconds or for centuries he landed on his oustretched arms in a sort of narrow crypt, its ceiling so low that he could only stand upright in it by thrusting his head into the opening by which he had entered. He explored it carefully with his hands. The floor was firm, smooth and strangely warm, but the walls presented astonishing irregularities. There were stony nipples and protuberances, mineral mushrooms, petrified sponges. Farther on the surface was covered with a tapestry of curled papillae which became rougher and thicker as he drew near a big mineral flower, a sort of limestone concretion, not unlike the sand-roses that are to be found in some deserts. A damp metallic smell emanated from this, comforting in its acidity, with a trace of sugared tartness recalling the sap of a fig-tree. But what attracted Robinson more than everything else was a cavity or recess about five feet deep which he found in the farthest corner of the crypt. Its walls were perfectly smooth but curiously shaped, like the interior of a mould designed to fashion some very complex object. The object, Robinson suspected, was his own body, and after a number of attempts he succeeded in finding a posture – knees drawn up to his chin, shins crossed, hands resting on his feet – which enabled him to fit so exactly into the recess that he forgot the limitations of his body directly he had adopted it.

He was suspended in a happy eternity. Speranza was a fruit ripening in the sun whose white and naked seed, embedded in a thousand thicknesses of skin and husk and rind, bore the name of Robinson. How to describe his sense of peace, installed in this most secret place, in the rocky intimacy of the unknown island? Had there ever before been a shipwreck on its shores, and a survivor of that shipwreck who, turning labourer and administrator, had covered its surface with crops and increased the herds in its fields? Or were those exploits no more than the dream without substance of this small, soft grub buried in the eternity of the huge vessel of stone? What was he, if not the very soul of Speranza? He recalled the wooden dolls of his childhood enclosed one within the other, each one hollow, and squeaking when one unscrewed it, except the last and smallest of all, which was solid and unbreakable, the nut, the reason for all the others.

Perhaps he slept. He could not have said. In the state of non-existence in which he found himself the difference between waking and sleeping was scarcely to be perceived.

When he racked his brains in an effort to determine how long had passed since his entry into the cave he was confronted, with a monotonous persistency, with the picture of the stopped water-clock. He noted one more occurrence of the flash of light denoting the passage of the sun across the axis of the cave, and it was shortly after this that an event occurred which surprised him, although he had long been expecting something of the kind. The darkness suddenly changed its nature. The blackness in which he was enveloped turned to white. He was floating in white shadow, like a lump of cream in a bowl of milk. And had he not been forced to rub his body with milk in order to penetrate to this depth?

In this deep place the feminine nature of Speranza became wholly maternal, and because the weakening of the bounds of time and space enabled Robinson to plunge as never before into the forgotten world of his childhood, he was haunted by the memory of his mother. He seemed to be clasped in her arms, a strong, high souled woman, but deeply reserved and not given to the display of sentiment. He could not recall her ever kissing his five brothers and sisters or himself. Yet she was by no means a monster of coldness and indeed in matters affecting her family was the most ordinary of women. He had seen her weep with joy at recovering a family heirloom which for months had been lost. He had seen her beside herself with grief when their father was struck down by a heart attack. And where her children were concerned she was a woman inspired, in the highest sense of the word. Being wholly devoted, like their father, to the Quaker form of belief, she denied the authority of Holy Writ no less than that of the Roman Church. To the outrage of her neighbours she regarded the Bible as a book which, though no doubt it was inspired by God, had been written and rewritten by human hands and grossly distorted by the vicissitudes of time and history. How much more pure and living than those faded texts, handed down through the centuries, was the spring of wisdom that she felt within herself! In it God spoke directly to His servant, and the Holy Spirit visited her with its divine light. Her duty as a mother was for her a natural part of this serene faith. In her dealings with her children there was something of infallibility which sustained them more surely than any display of affection. She never kissed them, but they read in her eyes that she knew everything about them, feeling their joys and sorrows even more acutely than they did themselves, and that in humbly serving them she drew upon an inexhaustible store of love, clear-sightedness and courage. The children were dismayed, when they visited neighbours, by the alternation of fury and fondness, cuffs and caresses, which the scolding, overworked women lavished on their offspring, whereas their own mother, always mistress of herself, imperturbably found the right word or gesture to soothe or rejoice their hearts.

One day when their father was away from the house fire had broken out in the shop on the ground floor. Their mother was with the children on the floor above. The fire had spread through the centuries-old wooden building with a terrifying rapidity. Robinson was then only a few weeks old, his oldest sister perhaps nine years. The cloth-merchant, hurriedly returning home, was on his knees in the street, praying that his family had somehow escaped when he saw his wife emerge calmly from the torrent of flames and smoke: like a tree bowed under the weight of its fruit, she was carrying her six uninjured children – in her arms, on her shoulders, on her back and clinging to her apron. It was thus that Robinson recalled his mother, a pillar of truth and goodness, a haven of comfort and strength, the refuge of his griefs and fears. And here in this rocky cavity he had rediscovered something of that flawless dry tenderness, that unfailing, undemonstrative solicitude. He saw again his mother's hands, big hands which neither fondled nor dealt blows, so strong, so sure, so shapely that they were like two angels, fraternal angels working together at the dictates of the spirit. He saw them kneading a paste of smooth, white dough, for it was the eve of Epiphany. Tomorrow the children would have a cake of special flour with beans concealed within its folds. He himself was that supple dough, caught in a hand of all-powerful stone. He was the bean, caught in the massive, indestructible flesh of Speranza.

The lightning-flash was again reflected down into the depths where he hung suspended, even more disembodied by fasting. But in the white darkness that enveloped him its effect seemed to Robinson to be reversed: for a fraction of a second the white turned black, then instantly regained its snowy purity. It was as though a wave of ink had flowed into the cave, instantly to recede, leaving no trace behind.

Robinson knew that he must break the spell if he was to see daylight again. Life and death were so close to one another in this shining place that it needed only a moment of inattention, a relaxing of the will to live, for him to slip from one into the other. He crawled out of the recess. He was not really either paralysed or weakened, but lightened, rather, and as it were spiritualized. He climbed without difficulty up the chimney, in which he now had room to spare. Having reached the end of the cave, he felt for his clothes and rolled them in a bundle under his arm without troubling to dress. The milky obscurity still surrounded him, and this caused him some apprehension. Had he lost his sight during his long sojourn underground? He was hesitatingly approaching the entrance when a sword of fire suddenly smote him. A searing pain assailed his eyes and he covered his face with his hands.

The midday sun was causing the air above the rocks to quiver. It was the hour when the very lizards look for shade. Robinson walked on, bent double, shivering with cold and pressing his thighs together, caked with curdled milk. His helpless exposure to the brambles and sharp pebbles filled him with alarm and shame. He was naked and white. His skin was goosefleshed like that of a frightened hedgehog that has lost its prickles. His penis had shrunk to nothing. From between his fingers came a shrill whimpering sound like the squeak of a mouse.

He made his way as best he could to the Residence, guided by Tenn, who danced around him in delight at his return but dismayed by his altered aspect. In the healing half-light of the house his first act was to start the water-clock again.

Journal

I am still far from being able to assess the value of my retreat in the heart of Speranza. Was it profit or loss? The answer would call for a long process of inquiry, for which the essential pieces are lacking. It must be said that the recollection of the mire causes me anxiety, since between it and the cave there is an undeniable affinity. But has not the evil thing always aped the good? Lucifer imitates God after his own fashion, which is a grimace. Is the cave a new and more alluring aspect of the mire, or is it its refutation? What is certain is that, like the mire, it recalls to my mind the ghosts of my past, and this retrospective dreaming is in no way appropriate to the daily struggle whereby I seek to bring Speranza to the highest possible state of civilization. But whereas the mire principally evoked the memory of my sister Lucy, a passing, tender fancy – morbid, in a word – the cave brings back the lofty and stern figure of my mother. A noble visitation! I am near to believing that that great spirit, seeking to aid the most imperilled of her children, has found no other way than by incarnating herself in Speranza, the better to sustain and cherish me. Certainly it was a harsh ordeal, the return to daylight even more than the burial in darkness. Yet in this beneficent discipline I seem to perceive the hand of my mother, to whom it was a matter of course that every achievement must be preceded, and in a sense paid for, by an arduous effort. And how I have been comforted by that period of retreat! My life now rests on a wonderfully solid basis; it is rooted in the very heart of the rock, directly in touch with the forces slumbering within it. Previously there had always been something insecure in me, an unbalance which was a source of mental sickness and distress. I sought to console myself with visions of a house, *the* house in which I would end my days, built massively of blocks of granite, resting on unshakable foundations. I indulge no longer in that dream. I no longer need it.

It is written that we cannot enter the Kingdom of Heaven except with the humility of a child. Never was any word of the Scriptures more literally true. The cave not only affords me the unshakable rock on which I may rest my poor life; it is a return to the lost innocence which all men secretly mourn. It unites as by a miracle the peace of the sweet maternal darkness and the peace of the grave, the one before, the other after life.

Robinson made several more retreats into the cave, but then was distracted by the needs of the hay and cereal harvest. Both were so scanty that he was alarmed. Although neither his personal provisioning nor that of his herds was in danger, since the island was sufficiently cultivated to sustain a much larger population, he had a sense of disequilibrium in the subtle relationship between himself and Speranza. It seemed to him that the new strength swelling his muscles, the springtide lightness of heart that caused him to break into a hymn of praise each morning when he rose, the renewed youth which he drew from the depths of the cave, were drawn from Speranza's own source of life and had dangerously diminished her most secret strength. The generous rains which ordinarily restored the earth after the heavy labour of the harvest were this year withheld in a leaden sky, shot with lightning-flashes and always lowering, but unyielding and dry. A plot of purslane which normally yielded a big supply of rich, juicy salad this year dried up without ripening. Several of the she-goats gave birth to stillborn kids. One day as a herd of wild pigs crossed the marshland on the eastern coast Robinson saw a cloud of dust rising above them, from which he concluded with profound satisfaction that the mire must have disappeared. But on the other hand the two springs from which he was accustomed to draw fresh water had dried up, and he had to go a long way into the forest to find another source of supply.

The new spring trickled weakly from a breast of earth rising in a clearing amid the trees, as though in this place the island had drawn aside her garment of forest. Robinson ran to it with a sense of wild rejoicing, and as he knelt down to suck the lifegiving draught the words of the Lord to Moses seemed to glow beneath his closed lids in letters of flame – 'I will lead you into a land flowing with milk and honey.'

But he could not conceal from himself the fact that although his own belly might be filled with milk and honey, Speranza was becoming exhausted by the monstrous maternal role he had imposed on her.

Journal

The matter is settled. Yesterday I again went down into the recess. It was the last time, for now I recognize my error. During the night, while I hung suspended in a half-sleep, my semen escaped me. I had only time to place my hand, for its protection, over the narrow crevice, no more than two fingers broad, at the very bottom of the womb of Speranza. The words of the Evangelist returned to me, but this time with a warning note: 'Except ye become as little children . . . ' By what aberration did I plume myself on possessing the innocence of a child? I am a man in the fullness of life and I should accept my manhood's destiny. The strength I drew from the womb of Speranza was the perilous price of a regression into the sources of myself. It is true that I there found peace and happiness, but with my man's weight I was crushing the earth that nurtured me. Being pregnant with myself, Speranza could no longer conceive, just as the menstrual flow dries up in a prospective mother. Even worse, I came near to sullying her with my semen. What hideous ripening might not that living seed have produced, in the dark, vast warmth of the cave? I think of Speranza swelling like a loaf in which the yeast is working, her bloated body spreading over the surface of the waters, eventually to die in disgorging some monster of incest!

At the peril of my soul, my life and the integrity of Speranza I had explored the intimate ways of the maternal earth. Perhaps later, when age has sterilized my body and sapped my virility, I may again go down to the recess. If I do so it will be never to re-emerge. Thus I shall have ensured to my remains the most loving and maternal of tombs.

The water-clock resumed its steady dripping and Robinson's tireless activities again filled the earth and sky of Speranza. He was carrying out a project which hitherto he had shirked, thinking it too vast for him to undertake: the conversion of the marshlands on the east coast of the island into rice-paddies. He had not touched the sack of rice since he brought it from the *Virginia*. To have consumed it without seeking to multiply it, squander in momentary self-indulgence the capital that might yield a hundred harvests, this to him was a crime – the crime of crimes – which he could not bring himself to commit, which indeed he would have been physically incapable of committing, for not a grain of the slaughtered seed would have passed his lips or been digested by his outraged stomach.

But the cultivation of rice required that the paddyfield should be flooded and drained as needed, which called for a system of water-conservation with its attendant ditches and sluices. It was a huge undertaking for a single man already burdened with other crops, livestock and official duties. For months the dripping of the water-clock never ceased, but Robinson's regularly kept journal testified to the progress of those meditations on life, death and sex which were no more than the surface-reflection of a metamorphosis in the depths of his being.

I know now that if the society of others is a fundamental element in the constitution of the human individual, it is nevertheless not irreplaceable. Necessary, yes: but not indispensable, as the Friends of George Fox said with humility of themselves. The companionship of his fellows may be replaced out of his own resources by the man whom circumstance has deprived of it. To replace the *given* by the *created* is a universal problem, and most especially a human problem if it be true that what sets man apart from the animals is his need to supply by his own endeavours those things which Nature bestows gratuitously on the beasts of the field — clothing, weapons, daily nourishment. Alone on my island I could sink to the level of the animals by creating nothing — which, indeed, is what I did at the outset — or become a kind of superman by creating the more because society gives me nothing. Therefore I have built, and I shall continue to build; but the truth is that my work proceeds on two different levels, and in *opposite directions*. For if on the surface of the island I pursue the work of civilization — tillage, stockbreeding, building, administering, law-giving — which follows the pattern of human society and is therefore in a sense retrospective, I feel that in myself I am the scene of a more radical process of creation, one which is engaged in finding new and original substitutes to fill the waste that solitude has created within me, all more or less tentative and so to speak experimental, but bearing less and less resemblance to the human model whence they sprang. It seems to be impossible that the growing divergence between these two opposed principles can continue indefinitely. Inevitably a time will come when an increasingly *dehumanized* Robinson will be incapable of being the governor and architect of an increasingly *humanized* estate. Already I am conscious of blank periods in my every-day activities. I find myself working without any real belief in what I am doing, and yet the quality and quantity of my work does not suffer from this. On the contrary, there are kinds of repetitive work which have everything to gain from absence of mind: we work for work's own sake, without thinking of the end in view. But one cannot continue indefinitely to hollow out a structure from within without its finally collapsing. The time must surely come when my ordered and cultivated island will wholly cease to interest me. It will then have lost its sole inhabitant.

Why then do I delay? Why not decide now that the time has come? Why? Because in the present state of my soul this would inexorably lead to my return to the mire. A world is being conceived within me. But a world in gestation is another name for chaos. Against this chaos the *ordered* island – ordered more and more rigorously because in this matter one cannot hold one's ground except by going forward – is my only safeguard, my only refuge. It has saved me and continues to do so every day. Meanwhile my inner world may continue in search of itself. Parts of the chaos are provisionally resolved. For example, I thought that in the cave I had found a workable solution. It was an error, but the experiment was useful. There will be others. I do not know where this progressive recreation of myself will eventually take me. If I know, it would mean that the process was ended, final and complete.

Thus with sexual desire. It is a torrent which Nature and Society have confined within a mill-race, a mill, a mechanism designed to serve an end with which in itself it is not concerned, the perpetuation of the species.

I have lost this outlet. With the social structure which during the years has crumbled to ruins within me, there has also perished the framework of institutions and myths which permits desire to become *embodied*, in the twofold sense of the word – that is to say, to assume a positive form and to expand itself in the body of a woman. To say that my sexual desire is no longer directed towards the perpetuation of the species is not enough. It no longer knows what its purpose is! For a long time memory was sufficiently active in me to feed my imagination with objects of desire, non-existent though they were. But that is now over. Memory has been sucked dry. The creatures of my imagination are lifeless shadows. I may speak the words, woman, breasts, thighs, thighs parted at my desire, but they mean nothing. Words have lost their image; they are sounds, no more. Does this mean that desire has died in me for lack of use? Far from it! I still feel within me that murmur of the spring of life, but it has become objectless. Instead of flowing submissively along the course set for it by society, it floods out in all

7

directions like the rays of a star, as though in search of a channel, the course wherein all the waters will be joined and flow together towards a goal.

It was this reflection that caused Robinson to become profoundly interested in the marital rites of the creatures surrounding him. He had always recoiled from observing the goats and vultures – in general, all mammals and birds – whose couplings seemed to him a repulsive caricature of human love. But the insects were well worthy of study. He knew that there were varieties which, foraging for nectar, picked up the pollen of the male flower and unconsciously conveyed it to the pistil of the female. The perfection of the process, as he watched it through a magnifying-glass in the case of a particular flower known in England as 'Dutchman's pipe', caused him to marvel. No sooner had a bee penetrated the slender corolla of the beautiful blossom than a reflex action caused it to close. The bee was thus held captive in the most exquisitely feminine of prisons. In struggling to escape it smothered its hairy legs with pollen, and then, being released by a second reflex, flew off to be imprisoned again elsewhere, the faithful and unknowing servitor of flowery loves.

This process of insemination at a distance, devised by the cruelly separated plants, seemed to Robinson both moving and supremely elegant, and he even dreamed of some fantastic variety of bird, which after charging itself with the seed of the Governor of Speranza, would fly to York to fecundate his deserted wife. But he reflected that being so long without news of him she must now consider herself a widow, if indeed she had not abandoned widowhood to marry again.

His meditations took another course. He became interested in the proceedings of a male hymenoptera which visited only one variety of orchid, and not, it seemed, for the purpose of foraging. Robinson spent long hours with his glass trying to determine what the creature was about. He noted first that the flower was an exact reproduction of the abdomen of the female insect, to the point of offering a sort of vagina which probably exuded a specific aphrodisiac scent calculated to attract and seduce the male. The insect did not rob the flower of its nectar; it *tickled* it, and then made love to it according to its own methods of propagation. In doing so its posture was such that the pollen contained in two sacs was deposited on its forehead, where it adhered to two sticky scales; and thus adorned with vegetable scales the deceived lover flew from male to female flower, serving the orchid species while it believed that it was doing its own business. This wonderful mingling of subterfuge and ingenuity was enough to make one doubt the sobriety of the Creator. Had the natural world been contrived by an infinitely wise and majestic God, or by a baroque demiurge driven to the wildest whimsicalities by his love of the bizarre? Repressing these doubts, Robinson reflected that there might be trees on the island which, like the orchids with the hymenoptera, might be disposed to make use of himself for the transference of their pollen. And the branches of the trees were transformed in his mind into voluptuous and scented women whose rounded bodies were waiting to receive him . . .

Searching the island from end to end, he finally discovered a quillaia, or quillai-tree, which had been blown over by the wind but not wholly uprooted. The trunk, which lay on the ground, ended in a fork of two main branches rising a little into the air. The bark was smooth and warm, even downy at the point of the fork, where there was a small aperture lined with silken moss.

Robinson hesitated for some days on the threshold of what he later called his 'vegetable way'. He hung about the quillai with sidelong glances, discovering in the two branches thrusting out of the grass a resemblance to huge, black, parted thighs. Finally he lay naked on the tree, clasping the trunk with his arms while his erect penis thrust its way into that mossy crevice. A happy torpor engulfed him. He lay dreaming with half-closed eyes of banks of creamy-petalled flowers shedding rich and heady perfumes from their bowed corollas. With damp lips parted they seemed to await the gift to be conferred on them by a heaven filled with the lazy drone of insects. Was he the last member of the human race to be summoned to return to the vegetable sources of life? The blossom is the sex of the plant. Innocently the plant offers its sex to all-comers as its most rare and beautiful possession. Robinson lay dreaming of a new human species which would proudly wear its male and female attributes on its head – huge, luminous, scented . . .

His liaison with quillai lasted several happy months. Then the rains came. Outwardly nothing was changed, but one day as he lay spread on his strange cross of love a searing pain in his gland brought him sharply to his feet. A big, red-spotted spider ran along the trunk of the tree and vanished into the grass. It was some hours before the pain abated, and his afflicted member looked like a tangerine.

Robinson had suffered many misadventures during his years of solitude amid the flora and fauna of a world enfevered by the tropical sun. But the moral significance of this episode was inescapable. Although it had been caused by the sting of a spider, could his malady be regarded as anything other than a venereal disease, the 'French sickness' against which his masters had so constantly warned him in his student days? He saw in this a sign that the 'vegetable way' might be no more than a dangerous blind alley.

Chapter 6

Robinson raised the stem of the sluice-gate three holes and secured it with a peg in the fourth. A tremor passed over the glassy surface of the freshwater reservoir and a green whirl-pool took shape, like the corolla of a flower, spinning with a gathering speed. A dead leaf drifting at the edge of the pool hung tentatively for an instant and was then sucked in. Robinson turned and stood with his back to the sluice-gate watching the carpet of muddy water as it crept over the flat patch of earth in a bubbling of dry grass, twigs and patches of foam. When it had reached the farther wall of the paddy, thirty yards on, the flow ceased and the level began to mount. An odour of decay and fruitfulness rose in the air. Robinson had selected that patch of alluvial land with its clay subsoil for the sowing of half his long-hoarded store of ten gallons of rice. The water would be maintained at the proper level until the flowering of the plants, and he would then allow it to sink and if necessary drain away completely while the ears ripened.

The gurgle of sluggishly moving water soaking into the earth, and the smell of stagnation, sharply evoked the memory of the mire. Robinson was torn between his triumph and a sense of sickening weakness. The rice-paddy represented the taming of the mire, a decisive victory over everything most primitive and disturbing in Speranza. But it was a victory that had been dearly won, and he would not easily forget the extreme effort it had cost him, the diversion of the stream to fill his artificial reservoir with its clean-cut clay walls, the digging of ditches, the building of the wooden barriers and the sluices lined at the bottom with stones to prevent erosion: all this in order that ten months hence – and after the husking, which in itself would take some weeks – a consignment of rice might be added to the wheat and barley with which his granary was already overflowing. Once again solitude condemned his toil in advance. He was suddenly and heart-rendingly conscious of the fruitlessness of his labours. What purpose did they serve, the tillage, the stockbreeding, the hoarding, the Charter, the Penal Code? Who was to be nourished by them, who protected? All was mockery, a defiance of reason. Everything he did, every task he undertook, was an appeal to some other person that met with no response.

Jumping the irrigation ditch he strode away, his eyes misty with despair. Why should he not destroy it all, burn the crops, blow up the buildings, open the enclosures and beat the goats so that they scattered in all directions? He imagined an earthquake shattering Speranza to fragments and the waters closing over that purulent crust of which he was the unhappy consciousness. He was convulsed with sobbing. Plunging through a copse of sandalwood and gum-trees, he reached a plateau of sandy grass and there flung himself on the ground, seeing nothing but the flash of lights in the red darkness behind his lids, hearing nothing but the tribulation that beat like a tempest in his veins.

It was not the first time, certainly, that the completion of a large task had left him empty and exhausted, a ready prey to despair; but he was beginning to feel more and more often that the cultivation of the island was a meaningless enterprise. It was at these moments that a new man seemed to be coming to life within him, wholly alien to the practical administrator. The two men did not yet co-exist in him; they came by turns, each excluding the other; and the danger was that the first of the two, the administrator, might vanish for good before the new man was fully grown.

Failing an upheaval there were tears, whose salt flow eventually dissolved the knot of exasperation and wretchedness that threatened to choke him. A gleam of sanity returned. He realized that in the ordering of the island lay his only salvation until such time as another kind of life – impossible to imagine, but which was groping to find itself within him – was ready to take the place of the wholly human course of behaviour which he had steadfastly pursued since the shipwreck. He must continue to labour while observing in himself the symptoms of his own metamorphosis.

He fell asleep. When he opened his eyes and rolled over on his back he found that the sun was setting. The breeze stirring the grass was like a sigh of compassion. Three pine trees were fraternally brushing their branches together as though in a gesture of consolation. Robinson felt his lightened spirit soar upward to where a great argosy of cloud sailed majestically across the sky. A wave of tenderness passed through him. And now it was that he felt the certainty of change – in the weight of the atmosphere, perhaps, or in the very breath of the world. He was in that *other island*, the one he had once glimpsed but had never seen again. He felt as never before that he was lying on Speranza as though on a living being, that the island's body was beneath him. Never before had he felt this with so much intensity, not even when he walked barefoot along the foreshore that so teemed with life. The almost carnal pressure of the island against his flesh warmed and excited him. She was naked, this earth that enveloped him, and he stripped off his own clothes. Lying with arms outstretched and a stirring in his loins, he embraced that great body burned all day by the sun which now exuded a musky sweat in the cooler air of the evening. He buried his face in the grass roots, breathing open-mouthed a long, hot breath. And the earth responded, filling his nostrils with the heavy scent of dead grass and the ripening of seed and the sap rising in new shoots. How closely and how wisely were life and death intermingled at this elemental level! His sex burrowed like a ploughshare into the earth, and overflowed in immense compassion for all created things. A strange wedlock, consummated in the vast solitude of the Pacific! He lay exhausted, the man who had married the earth, and it seemed to him, clinging timorously like a small frog to the skin of the terrestrial globe, that he was swinging vertiginously with her through infinite space . . . Finally, a little giddy, he got to his feet, and stood for a moment in the breeze, receiving the warm obeisance of the three pine trees whose silent applause was distantly echoed by the waving green crests of the forest fringing the horizon.

He was standing in a gently rolling meadow broken by folds and slopes dressed in a covering of round-stemmed, pink-tinted grass that was like a coat of hair. 'It's a combe,' he murmured to himself. 'A pink combe.' And this word vaguely suggested another to his mind, somehow related to it, which seemed to endow it with a new and far richer significance; but he could not recall the other word. He stood seeking to retrieve it from the well of forgetfulness in which it had long been buried. Combe . . . combe . . . comb. A comb. He had a sudden vision of a comb in a woman's hair, and then of hair flowing down the naked back of a woman running a little to fat but still majestic in her bearing. There was a swell of muscle round her shoulder-blades and below this the smooth expanse of flesh narrowed and was then thrust outward in a firm and gently rounded hillock divided by a central fold and covered by a hint of golden down. The woman turned smiling to face him and he saw the soft curve of her belly, the triangle at the meeting of her thighs, the offer of her loins. Her loins. The word came suddenly to Robinson, and it was the word he had been seeking. The loins . . . His hand resting on that tufted mound within which were stored the cravings of release and spasm, the heat, the

ardour and the essence, the well of human kind . . . The loins
. . . He turned and went back to the Residence with the word
singing in his ears.

Journal

The kind of *amazement* with which we open our eyes in the morning! Nothing better testifies to the fact that sleep is an experience
in its own right and as it were a rehearsal of death. Of all the
things that can happen to the sleeper, awakening is certainly the
one he least expects and the one for which he is least prepared. No
nightmare can so greatly dismay him as that sudden return to light,
another light. There can be no doubt that for the sleeper the act
of sleeping is final. The soul has taken flight from his body without
a backward look or thought of return. It has forgotten everything,
cast everything aside, when suddenly and harshly it is compelled
to resume the discarded garment of flesh, its habits and its life . . .
    So presently I shall lie down and let myself slip into the shades
for ever. A strange alienation. The sleeper is a mind unhinged that
thinks itself dead.

    The problem of existence. If someone had told me a few years
ago that the absence of my fellows would cause me to doubt my
own existence I would have laughed, just as I did when 'universal
consent' was offered as a proof of the existence of God. 'The
majority of men at all times and in all places have believed in the
existence of God. Therefore God exists.' How absurd! The most
absurd of all the proofs of the existence of God, miserably insuffi-
cient compared with that marvel of force and subtlety, the ontolo-
gical argument.
    But now I know otherwise. I know that universal consent is the
only proof – and not only of the existence of God.
    To exist – what do the words mean? It means to be outside –
sistere ex. That which is outside exists. That which is within does
not exist. My thoughts, images and dreams do not exist. If Speranza is no more than a sensation, or bundle of sensations, then she
does not exist. And I myself exist only in so far as I escape from
myself to join with others.

What complicates the position is that the thing which does not exist does its utmost to persuade us of the contrary. There is a great and universal urge towards existence among the non-existent. Something like a centrifugal force seeks to spread outward everything that moves within me, images, dreams, projects, fantasies, desires, obsessions. That which does not *ex-sist in-sists*. It insists upon existing. All the small world contained within me is knocking at the door of the great, the real world. And it is others, those who are outside, who hold the key. In the past, when I tossed in my sleep, my wife would shake me by the shoulders to wake me and dispel the *insistence* of the nightmare. But now . . . But why do I keep returning to this subject?

All those who knew me, all without exception, believe me dead. My own belief in my existence is opposed to that unanimous belief. No matter what I do, I cannot prevent that picture of Robinson's dead body from existing in all their minds. This alone, though certainly it does not kill me, suffices to remove me to the uttermost confines of life, to a place hung between Heaven and Hell – in a word, to Limbo. Speranza, or the Limbo of the Pacific . . .

This state of half-death at least helps me to understand the deep, positive and seemingly ineluctable relationship between sex and death. Being closer to death than any other man, I am by the same token closer to the very springs of sexuality.

Sex and death . . . Their close association was first made clear to me in the dissertations of Samuel Gloaming, an elderly York eccentric, a herbalist and taxidermist, whom I visited now and then of an evening in his shop filled with stuffed animals and dried herbs. He had devoted a lifetime's thought to the mysteries of creation, and he said that life was fragmented into an infinite number of entities differing as widely as possible, each from the other, so that it might have a no less infinite chance of surviving the vicissitudes of its environment. Were the earth to be frozen to a block of ice, or burned by the sun to a desert of stone, most of the creatures on its surface would perish, but thanks to their variety a few would still remain, capable of adapting themselves to the changed conditions. It was this multiplicity of creatures which in his view made reproduction necessary, that is to say, the transference of life from the old to the new; and he insisted that this was a sacrifice of the individual to the species, since in the act of procreation the individual loses something of his substance. Thus sexuality is the living presence, ominous and mortal, of the species in the essence of the individual. To procreate is to bring forth a new generation which innocently but inexorably will thrust its predecessor towards extinction. No sooner do the parents cease to be indispensable than they begin to become burdensome. The child casts aside his parents as naturally as he took from them all that he needed for his growth. The instinct which brings the sexes together is then an instinct of death. But Nature has thought it prudent to disguise her stratagem, transparent though it is, and what appears to be the self-indulgence of lovers is in reality a course of mad self-abnegation.

I had been pondering these matters when I had occasion to visit a part of northern Ireland which was grievously afflicted by famine. The survivors strayed like ghostly skeletons along the village streets, and the bodies of the dead were burned on pyres to guard against the risk of plague, more deadly than the famine itself. Most of the corpses were male, so true is it that women are capable of greater endurance than men, and they told a strange story: emaciated though they were, drained of substance like leathern dolls of string and bone, the sexual organ, and this alone, was monstrously and ironically enlarged, more rigid and distended, in a word more triumphant, than probably it had ever been in life. This apotheosis in death of the genitals shed an added light on Samuel Gloaming's words, evoking in my mind a dialogue between the individual, the affirmation of life, and sex, the affirmation of death. By the light of day man in his right mind represses what is undesirable, he diminishes and disdains it; but under the influence of darkness, warmth and languour the enemy revives, unsheaths his sword and diminishes the man, makes of him a lover, plunges him into a brief ecstasy, then closes his eyes – and the lover, couched on earth, lost in the rapture of forgetfulness and renunciation of self, sinks into that little death which is sleep.

Couched on earth . . . Those words, flowing naturally from my pen, are perhaps the key. Earth irresistibly draws the enclasped lovers with joined lips, cradling them after their embrace in the happy slumber of sensual delight. But earth also harbours the dead, sucks their blood and devours their flesh, that these orphans be restored to the cosmos from which for the length of a lifetime they were parted. Love and death, two aspects of the defeat of the individual, turn with a common impulse to the earth. Both are of their nature earthly.

The most sagacious among men are conscious of this relationship, though they may not clearly perceive it. To me in my unique situation it is crystal-clear, indeed I am forced in my entire being to live it. Lacking a woman, I am reduced to *immediate* loves. Deprived of that fruitful byway which a woman's body affords, I must turn directly to the earth which will be my last resting-place. What happened in the pink combe? I dug my grave with my sex and died the transient death that we call pleasure. And I note that in doing so I have accomplished a further stage in the metamorphosis I am undergoing. For it has taken me years to reach this point. When I was cast ashore I was still a creature moulded by society. The mechanism which directs sex from its natural tendency towards the earth to the living sheath of a woman, was still active in my loins. I wanted a woman or nothing. But solitude has simplified me. Since that byway is closed, the mechanism has become obsolete, and in the pink combe my sexuality returned to its source of origin, the earth. Moreover, this further stage in my dehumanization occurred at the very moment when my *alter ego* had completed, in the building of the rice-paddy, the most ambitious human project I have embarked on since I came to rule over Speranza.

How fascinating this tale would be were not I its sole protagonist, and if I did not write it in blood and tears!

Thou shalt also be a crown of glory in the hand of the Lord, and a royal diadem in the hand of thy God.

Thou shalt no more be termed Forsaken; neither shall thy land any more be termed Desolate; but thou shalt be called Hephzibah and thy land Beulah: for the Lord delighteth in thee, and thy land shall be married   Isaiah LXII

Standing at his lectern in the doorway of the Residence,

with the open Bible before him, Robinson recalled that in the distant past he had named the island Desolation. But this morning shone with a nuptial splendour, and Speranza lay prostrate at his feet in the tenderness of the rising sun. A herd of goats were coming down a hillside, and the kids, delighting in the slope and the press of life within them, were leaping and skipping like bouncing balls. To the west, the golden sweep of a field of ripe wheat swayed under the caress of a warm breeze. A cluster of palms half-hid the silvery glitter of a rice-paddy dotted with young shoots. The great cedar by the mouth of the cave sang with an organ-note. Robinson turned the pages of the Book of Books, and what he now read was no other than the love-song of Speranza and her spouse.

Behold, thou art fair, my love; behold, thou art fair; thou hast doves' eyes within thy locks: thy hair is as a flock of goats that appear from mount Gilead.

Thy teeth are like a flock of sheep that are even shorn, which came up from the washing; whereof every one bear twins, and none is barren among them.

Thy lips are like a thread of scarlet, and thy speech is comely: thy temples are like a piece of pomegranate within thy locks.

Thy neck is like the tower of David builded for an armoury, whereon there hang a thousand bucklers, all shields of mighty men.

Thy two breasts are like two young roes that are twins, which feed among the lilies.

And Speranza replied:

My beloved is gone down into his garden, to the beds of spices, to feed in the gardens, and to gather lilies.

I am my beloved's, and my beloved is mine: he feedeth among the lilies.

Thou art beautiful, O my love, as Tirzah, comely as Jerusalem, terrible as an army with banners.

I went down into the garden of nuts to see the fruits of the valley, and to see whether the vine flourished, and the pomegranates budded.

Or ever I was aware, my soul made me like the chariots of Amminadib.

And finally she said, as though in answer to his meditation on sex and death:

Set me as a seal upon thine heart, as a seal upon thine arm: for love is strong as death . . .

Thus Speranza was henceforth endowed with words. There was no longer only the rustle of the wind in the trees, or the surge of the unresting sea or the peaceful crackle of the night-fire with its twin reflection in the eyes of Tenn. The Bible, with its imagery identifying the woman with the earth, the wife with the garden, graced their love with the most ancient of epithalamia. Before long Robinson had all the burning lines by heart, and as he walked through the wood of gum-trees and sandalwood on his way to the pink combe he spoke the words of the husband and was silent while he listened to the wife's reply. Then he was ready to fling himself into a fold of sand and, setting Speranza like a seal upon his heart, appease in her his anguish and his desire.

Nearly a year passed before he perceived that his love was bringing about a change in the vegetation of the pink combe. He had taken no notice at first of the disappearance of grasses and small seedlings from the places where his own seed was sown. But his attention was caught by the growth of a new plant that he had seen nowhere else on the island. This plant had large, lace-edged leaves which grew in clusters at the level of the earth on a very short stalk. It bore white, sharp-scented blossoms with pointed petals and brown, ample berries which largely overflowed their calices.

Robinson observed them curiously but thought no more

about them until the day when it became unmistakably apparent that they appeared within a few weeks at the precise place where he had sown his seed. Thereafter he ceaselessly pondered the mystery. He sowed his seed in the earth near the cave, but to no avail. It seemed that these plants could grow nowhere but in the pink combe. Their strangeness restrained him from plucking and dissecting and tasting them as he might otherwise have done. He sought to dismiss the riddle from his mind, since it seemed to have no answer; but sudden light was shed by a verse from the *Song of Songs* which he had repeated a thousand times without attaching any special importance to it. '*The mandrakes give a smell,*' sang the young wife, '*and at our gates are all manner of pleasant fruits, new and old, which I have laid up for thee, O my beloved.*' Could it be that Speranza was keeping that Biblical promise? He had heard of the miracle of the plants, such as nightshade, which grow at the foot of gibbets, where the hanged have let fall their last drops of semen, and which are held to be the fruit of the crossing of man with earth. On the day when this thought occurred to him he ran to the pink combe and, kneeling beside one of the plants, very gently lifted it out of the ground, digging round the root with his hands. It was true! His love-making with Speranza was not sterile. The white, fleshy, curiously forked root bore an undeniable resemblance to the body of a woman-child. Trembling with delight and tenderness he put the mandrake back and pressed the earth round it as one puts a child to bed. Then he walked away on tiptoe, taking great care not to crush any of the other plants.

Thenceforward, blessed by the Bible, a stronger and more intimate bond united him with Speranza. He had humanized her whom he could henceforth call his wife in a manner that went incomparably deeper than all the enterprises of the Governor. That this closer union represented a further step in the shedding of his human self was something of which he was certainly aware, but he did not measure its extent until he perceived when he awoke one morning that his beard, growing in the night, had begun to take root in the earth.

Chapter 7

'Do not waste time, it is the stuff of life.'

Seated in a sort of sling made of lianas, Robinson thrust himself away from the rock-face on which he had painted these words. The letters stood out bold and white against the granite surface. The site was particularly favourable. Every word seemed to be hurled in a noiseless shout at the haze of the horizon fringing the vast glitter of the sea. During recent months the chance play of his memory had brought back tags from Benjamin Franklin's *Poor Richard's Almanack*, which his father held to be the quintessence of moral wisdom and had made him learn by heart. Stakes of wood planted in the sand-dunes proclaimed that 'Poverty robs a man of all virtue: it is hard for an empty sack to stand upright;' and encrusted in the wall of the cave was a sort of mosaic which read: 'If lying is the second vice, the first is indebtedness: for lies ride on the back of debts.' But the greatest of these aphorisms was destined to blaze in letters of fire on the beach, on some night when Robinson felt impelled to defy the dark-ness with a flaming assertion of truth. Pine-cones wrapped in tow, ready for lighting, were arranged on stones in a pattern which proclaimed: 'If knaves knew all the advantages of virtue they would turn virtuous out of knavery.'

The island was covered with fields of cereal and vegetables, the rice-paddy would soon be yielding its first harvest, the goat-pens were filled and the cave overflowed with a store of foodstuffs sufficient to maintain the population of a village for several years. Yet for Robinson the magnificent achieve-

8

ment was being inexorably drained of its content. The cultivated island was losing its soul as it gave way to *the other island*, so that it resembled a great machine spinning in a vacuum. This had caused him to reflect that the cultivated isle, fostered with such prudent economy, might yield a system of morals of which the principles were laid down in Master Franklin's writings; and so he had set about inscribing these on stone and earth and wood, in the very flesh of Speranza, to endow her great body with a soul that suited it.

Carrying his goathair brush in one hand, and in the other the pot of fine-ground chalk liquefied with holly-sap, Robinson set out to find a suitable site for yet another aphorism, seemingly materialistic but affirming a certain mastery over time – 'He who kills a sow destroys her progeny unto the thousandth generation; he who squanders a crown-piece destroys a mountain of sovereigns.'

A herd of goats fled in disorder at his approach. It would be amusing, he reflected, to paint the sentence on 113 goats, one letter to each goat, leaving it to hazard to determine when, in the course of their endless permutations, they would arrange themselves in the right order and reveal the message. He was toying with this notion, and trying to reckon the mathematical odds, when suddenly he let fall his brush and paint-pot, and stood rigid with alarm. A column of white smoke was rising into the clear sky. It came, as on the previous occasion, from the Bay of Salvation, and it had the same thick, milky quality. But this time the messages painted on the rock face and arranged in the dunes and on the beach would warn the intruders of an alien presence, and they might come in search of him. Followed by Tenn, Robinson ran for the fortress, praying that they had not got there before him. An incident occurred during his panic flight which at the time he scarcely noticed, but which later he recalled as a fateful omen. One of the tamest of his billy-goats, startled by his rapid movement, lowered its head and charged him.

Robinson just managed to avoid it, but Tenn was knocked howling into a clump of fern.

They reached the fortress to find it undisturbed; but what Robinson had not foreseen was the effect on his nerves of the possibility of an attack. The place where the Araucanians had landed was less than a mile away. If they were already moving to attack him they would have the advantage of surprise as well as of numbers. On the other hand, they might be so preoccupied with their murderous ceremonies as to have paid no attention to the signs that the island was inhabited. The uncertainty was intolerable. He had to know. Accordingly he took down a musket, thrust the pistol into his belt, and, still followed by Tenn, who was now limping, plunged into the undergrowth in the direction of the bay. Then he was obliged to hurry back, having forgotten his spyglass.

There were again three outrigger canoes drawn up on the beach, looking from above like children's toys; but the number of men encircling the fire was larger than on the previous occasion, and it seemed to Robinson, studying them through the glass, that they did not belong to the same tribal group. To judge by the heap of quivering flesh over which two executioners were standing, the ritual had already passed its climax. But then something occurred which looked like a departure from the customary procedure. The witch-doctor, springing suddenly to her feet from her crouching position, darted towards one of the men in the circle and pointed to him with a skinny arm, her mouth opening in a flood of imprecations which Robinson could not hear. Clearly she was demanding a second sacrifice. There was a stir in the circle of men, and the executioners, *machete* in hand, approached this new offender, who was flung to the ground by the men on either side of him. A *machete* flashed, cutting away the leather apron which was his only garment. The blade rose again, preparing to descend on his naked body, but as it did so the victim leapt to his feet and made a dash for the trees. Through the spyglass he appeared to be simply leaping in the air with the two executioners behind him; but in fact he was running with remarkable speed, straight in Robinson's direction. Although he was no taller than the rest, he was very much more slender, and built on more athletic lines. He was also darker-skinned and somewhat negroid in feature, in general different from the other men, and it may have been this which had caused him to be singled out for sacrifice.

He drew rapidly nearer, steadily increasing the distance between himself and his pursuers. Had Robinson not been certain that he was well-hidden he might have supposed that the man had seen him and was coming to him for help. He had to make up his mind. In another minute he would be confronted by all three Indians, who might be reconciled among themselves by the sudden appearance of another potential victim. And at this moment Tenn set up a furious barking. The infernal animal! Robinson seized hold of him, and with an arm round his neck, holding his mouth shut with his left hand, he strove awkwardly to level his musket with the other. He was faced now by a moral problem. If he shot down one of the pursuers he might rouse the whole tribe against him. On the other hand, if he shot the sacrificial victim it might be interpreted as a supernatural act, the intervention of an outraged divinity. He had to take one side or the other, being indifferent to both, and prudence counselled that he should support the stronger. He aimed at the breast of the fugitive, who was now very close, but at the moment of firing Tenn, making a sudden effort to get free, diverted his aim. It was the first of the pursuers who staggered and fell to the ground. The man behind him stopped, bent over the dying body, stared blankly for a moment at the trees and finally turned and fled wildly back to his companions.

Crouched in a clump of tree-fern, a naked and panic-stricken black man pressed his forehead to the ground, while with one hand he groped for the foot of a bearded and armed white man, clad in goatskin and a bonnet of fur, accoutred with the trappings of three thousand years of western civilization, and sought to place it on his neck.

Robinson and the Araucanian passed the night within the battlements of the fortress, intently listening to the sighs and murmurs of the forest, as loud by night as they were by day, although they were different. Every two hours Robinson sent Tenn out to reconnoitre, his duty being to bark if he detected any human presence. But each time he returned without having given the alarm. The Araucanian, who was wearing an old pair of sailor's trousers which Robinson had made him put on less as a protection against the cold than from his own sense of propriety, was mute and apathetic, seemingly oppressed both by the narrowness of his escape and the extraordinary place in which he found himself. He had not touched the wheat-cake Robinson had offered him, but he constantly chewed some sort of wild berry, causing Robinson to wonder how he had come by them. Shortly before daylight he fell asleep on a pile of dead leaves, curled up surprisingly with Tenn, who was also exhausted. Robinson knew that some Chilean natives were in the habit of using a domestic animal to warm them in the chill of the tropic nights, but he was nevertheless surprised at the readiness with which the dog, generally shy and timid, had accepted this procedure.

Perhaps the Indians were waiting until daylight to attack. Armed with his pistol, both muskets and all the powder and ball he could carry, Robinson set out from the fortress and reached the Bay of Salvation by way of a wide detour through the sand-dunes. The foreshore was deserted. The three canoes and their occupants had gone, taking with them the body of the man he had shot. Nothing remained but the black circle of the ritual fire in which the human bones were scarcely distinguishable from the sticks of charred wood. In the act of dropping his assortment of weapons and ammunition on the sand, Robinson found that he had rid himself of all the accumulated terrors of the night. He was shaken by a great burst of uncontrollable, nervous laughter, and when at length he recovered his breath he reflected that it was the first time he had laughed since the wreck of the *Virginia*. Was this the first result of his having acquired a companion? Had the gift of laughter been restored to him with the return of human society, on however modest a scale? He was to return to that question, but at this moment another thought occurred to him, very much more momentous. The *Escape*. He had always avoided the scene of that disastrous failure, which had been the prelude to his period of total collapse. Nevertheless the *Escape* was still there, waiting, with her bow pointing to the sea, for arms strong enough to launch her. Perhaps with the newcomer's aid he would be able to complete that long-abandoned venture, and the youth's knowledge of the archipelago would be invaluable.

Returning to the fortress, Robinson found the Araucanian stripped naked and playing with Tenn. This shamelessness irritated him, as did the friendship that seemed to have sprung up between the boy and the dog. After bluntly indicating that he must put his trousers on, Robinson led him to the clearing where he had built the *Escape*.

The broom had grown so high that the squat little craft looked as though it were afloat on a sea of yellow blossom rippling in the breeze. The mast had fallen, and here and there the deck-planking bulged, doubtless under the influence of rain and sun; but otherwise the hull seemed to be intact. Tenn, who had run ahead, bounded round the vessel several times, disclosing his presence in the bushes only by the stir of butterflies that marked his course. He jumped suddenly on to the deck, and instantly it collapsed beneath him. Robinson saw him vanish with a startled yelp into the bottom of the hull. Drawing nearer he saw the rest of the deck-planking give way each time Tenn attempted to scramble out. The Araucanian seized hold of the edge of the hull, and raising his closed fist opened it under Robinson's nose, allowing a handful of reddish powder to be borne away on the wind. He was laughing. Robinson gave the hull a gentle kick and a cloud of dust rose in the air while a hole appeared in the boat's side. The termites had done their work. The *Escape* was little more than a heap of sawdust.

Journal

So many bitter disappointments during the past three days, and so many mortifying setbacks to my pride! God has sent me a companion, but by some freak of the Divine Wisdom He has elected to choose one from the lowest stratum of humanity. Not only is the man coloured, a coastal Araucanian, but he is clearly not of pure blood. Everything about him points to the half-caste, a South-American Indian crossed with Negro. If he had even attained the age of reason and were capable of appreciating his own insignificance in face of the civilization I represent! But I should be surprised if he is more than fifteen years old, bearing in mind the extreme precocity of these inferior races, and his childishness moves him to impertinent laughter when I seek to instruct him.

Moreover, this unforeseen incursion into the long years of my solitude has shattered my fragile equilibrium. The *Escape* has again occasioned me a humiliating moral collapse. Despite all the years of sowing and reaping, breeding, building, ordering, law-giving, it needed only the faintest gleam of hope to set me plunging towards the deadly trap in which I once so nearly succumbed. I must take note of the warning in a spirit of humble acceptance. I have grieved long enough over the absence of the human companionship for which all my work on the island has been a vain appeal. That companionship has now been vouchsafed me in its most primitive and rudimentary form, but this will at least make it the easier for me to mould it to my requirements. My course is clear. I must fit my slave into the system which I have perfected over the years. My success in doing so will be manifest on the day when there can no longer be a doubt that Speranza and he have jointly benefited from their meeting. I had to find a name for the newcomer. I did not choose to give him a Christian name until he was worthy of that dignity. A savage is not wholly a human being. Nor could I in decency give him an invented name, although this would perhaps have been the sensible solution. I think I have solved the problem with some elegance in giving him the name of the day on which I saved him – Friday. It is the name neither of a person nor of a common object but somewhat between the two, that of a half-living, half-abstract entity, a name strongly stressing its temporal character, fortuitous and as it were episodic . . .

Friday rapidly acquired enough English to be able to understand his master's orders. He learnt to plough and sow and reap, to thresh and winnow, grind and cook. He milked the goats, made cheese, collected turtles' eggs and soft-boiled them, dug ditches, saw to the fishponds, trapped vermin, caulked the canoe, mended his master's garments and polished his boots. In the evening, clad in a serving-man's livery, he waited at the Governor's table. Then he warmed his bed and helped him to undress, before himself retiring to the litter which he placed by the doorway of the Residence and shared with Tenn.

Friday was utterly docile. The truth is that his spirit had died at the moment when the witch-doctor pointed her finger at him, and what had fled for safety was a body without a soul, as blind and unwitting as a duck that runs with flapping wings after its head has been cut off. But the body had not run aimlessly. It had run in search of its soul, which was in the hands of a white man. Since then Friday had belonged body and soul to the white man. All that his master ordered was right, all that he forbade was wrong. It was good to toil night and day for the functioning of an elaborate system that served no purpose; it was bad to eat more than the portion allotted to him by his master. It was good to be a soldier when his master was a general, a choir-boy when his master prayed, a builder's labourer when he built, a farm-labourer when he farmed, a herdsman when he herded, a beater when he hunted, a paddler when he travelled by water, a bedside attendant when he was sick, an operator of the fan and a killer of flies. It was wrong to smoke a pipe, to go naked, or to hide when there was work to be done. Friday's good-will was boundless, but on the other hand he was very young and there were times when youth was too much for him. Then he would laugh. He would burst into an explosion of laughter, confounding the Governor, the sober-minded mentor, the administrator of the island, and putting him out of countenance. Robinson detested those youthful outbursts, which threw his order into confusion and undermined his authority. It was Friday's laughter which first moved Robinson to strike him. Friday was required to repeat after him the religious and moral axioms which he propounded in measured tones. For example – 'God is an all-powerful, omniscient master, infinitely good, merciful and just, the Creator of Man and of All Things.' And Friday's laugh rang out, irrepressible, lyrical and blasphemous, to be extinguished like a snuffed candle by a resounding blow on the cheek. This image of a merciful, all-powerful God had seemed to him irresistibly comic in the light of his own brief experience of life. But no matter; in a voice now trembling with sobs he dutifully repeated his master's words.

And he afforded the Governor one source of particular satisfaction. Thanks to him, Robinson could now find a use for the money he had saved from the wreck. He paid Friday. He paid him a wage of a half-sovereign a month. In the first instance he merely 'invested' the money for him, allowing it to accumulate at the rate of five per cent; but later, considering him to have attained the age of reason, he handed it over to him with the accumulated arrears. Friday could spend the money on extra rations, small objects of use, trifles brought from the *Virginia,* or simply on buying himself a half-day's repose (a whole day was not purchasable) which he spent in the hammock he had made for himself.

For although Sunday was officially a day of rest, it was not a day of culpable idleness. Rising at dawn, Friday swept and garnished the Meeting House. Then he woke his master and recited the morning prayer with him; following which they repaired together to the Meeting House, there to join in a ceremony of worship after the Quaker fashion lasting two hours. Standing at the lectern, the master read passages from the Scriptures interrupted by long periods of meditation and enlightened with commentaries inspired by the Holy Spirit. Kneeling on the left side of the hall, the right being reserved for women, Friday listened devoutly to words such as *sin, salvation, hell-fire, damnation, Mammon* and *apocalypse* which if they conveyed no precise meaning to his mind nevertheless had a magical effect, one of obscure, disturbing beauty. And now and then a picture would emerge – for example, of a man swallowed by a whale who escaped unscathed, of a country beset by a plague of frogs so numerous that they were to be found in the beds and even in the loaves, and of a herd of swine which rushed into the sea, being possessed by devils. On these occasions Friday would feel a tickling in his throat and mirth welling up inside him. With a great effort he would concentrate his mind on suitably dismal subjects, for he dared not think what would happen if he burst out laughing during the Sunday meeting.

After luncheon, which was a longer, more elaborate meal than on weekdays, the Governor, carrying a stick he had made for himself which bore some resemblance to a monarch's sceptre, and with his head shaded by a huge goatskin parasol carried by Friday, would make a tour of the island, inspecting his fields, rice-paddies, orchards and herds, his completed works and works in progress, bestowing praise and blame on his follower together with instructions regarding next week's schedule. Since the remaining hours of the day, like those preceding them, could not be devoted to any form of productive employment, Friday made use of these to tidy and embellish the island. He weeded pathways, planted flowers outside the buildings and trimmed the trees that graced the residential quarter. By dissolving beeswax in essence of terebinth coloured with dyer's oak Robinson had produced a handsome polish for which in the past he had found little use, since furniture was scarce and wood floors non-existent on the island. It now occurred to him that Friday might use it to polish the flags and cobbles forming the surface of the island's main thoroughfare, the pathway running from the cave to the Bay of Salvation which he had followed on his first day. The pathway's importance as a historical monument seemed to him on reflection to justify the immense labour involved, although the polish would be washed away by the first shower of rain and he had at first had some doubts about ordering Friday to undertake the task.

Friday had gained his master's approval with several fortunate contrivances of his own. One of Robinson's problems had always been to dispose of his kitchen waste in such a fashion as not to attract the notice of the vultures and rats. None of the methods he had tried had been wholly satisfactory. The rats dug up anything he buried, the tides flung back whatever he dumped in the sea, and burning meant that the stuff had to be carried some distance if the smoke of the bonfire was not to pervade the living quarters. Friday's method was to make use of a colony of red ants whose termitary was only a stone's throw from the Residence. Seen at a distance, the garbage deposited on the anthill seemed to be endowed with a quivering life of its own and it was fascinating to watch viscera and skin and gristle disappear until nothing was left but the cleanly stripped bones.

Friday also showed himself to be adept in the use of the bolas, that species of sling consisting of two or three stones on separate cords joined by a central knot, which, properly handled, can be made to fly through the air like a spinning wheel and wrap itself round anything it encounters. At first he used it simply for catching the goats for milking, but it was also useful for bringing down animals for the pot. Eventually he persuaded Robinson that by the use of larger stones it could be made into an effective weapon of offence, capable of immobilizing and even half-strangling an enemy if it caught him in the right place. Haunted by the fear of another Araucanian invasion, Robinson was delighted to add the simple device to his armoury, and they spent hours practising with it on the foreshore, using for target a tree-stump the size of a man.

Thus during the period immediately following Friday's arrival the cultivated island became of necessity Robinson's main preoccupation, as for the time being he devoted himself to his functions as Governor, Commander-in-Chief and Spiritual Pastor. He even believed for a while that the newcomer would provide a justification of his material ordering of things, a weight and stability that would finally dispose of the dangers with which solitude had threatened him, in much the way that some ships are not fully seaworthy until ballasted with a certain amount of cargo. He went so far as to consider another possible danger arising out of the state of permanent tension in which the inhabitants of the island lived, and the immense supply of victuals which overflowed their store-rooms. He wondered whether he should counteract this by instituting a regular system of high-days at which there would be feasting and drinking. But he suspected that this idea, which accorded so ill with the true spirit of the cultivated island, was subconsciously inspired by his longing for 'the other island', which was temporarily in abeyance but secretly growing stronger within him. Perhaps it was this nostalgia which prevented him from being wholly content with Friday's docility and impelled him to drive and test him to the uttermost limit.

Journal

He obeys me implicitly in everything, and it is strange that I should still find cause for complaint. But in his very submission there is something too complete, something almost automatic, which chills me – apart from the dumbfounding laughter which at moments he seems unable to control, and which is like the sudden manifestation of a devil within him. A devil. Yes, Friday is possessed. Indeed, he is doubly possessed, for I must acknowledge that, except for those bursts of demonic laughter, it is I who ordain his every thought and deed.

I do not look for much reason in a man of colour – of mixed colour, I should say, since he is both Indian and Negro. But at the least he might show affection, and except for his absurd and rather shocking fondness for Tenn I can discover in him no sign at all of human warmth. I am troubled by a regret which it is painful to avow but which I am bound to set down. I would never venture to say to him 'Love me', because I know all too well that for the first time I should not be obeyed. Yet he has no reason not to love me. I saved his life – unintentionally, it is true, but how can he know that? I have taught him everything, and above all to work, which is our greatest wealth. Certainly I beat him from time to time, but he must surely know that it is for his own good. Yet his behaviour in this matter is sometimes disconcerting. One day when I was showing him, rather impatiently perhaps, how to peel and split willow-shoots before plaiting them, I made a somewhat sweeping gesture with my hand. To my great astonishment he sprang backwards, covering his face with his arm. But it would have been senseless in me to strike him at a moment when I was trying to teach him a difficult skill calling for the closest application on his part. Alas, everything leads me to suppose that in his eyes, and at every moment of the day and night, I am prompted by that kind

125

of unreason. Putting myself in his place, I am filled with pity for this defenceless boy, cast upon a desert island at the mercy of a lunatic. But my own state is even worse, for I see my unnatural reflection in the gaze of my sole companion as though in a distorting mirror.

Weary of watching him mechanically obey my orders, without apparently having any interest in the reason for them, I resolved to carry the matter to its logical conclusion. I set him a task which in every prison in the world is held to be the last extreme of futility and degradation – the task of digging a hole and filling it in with the contents of a second; then digging a third, and so on. He laboured at this for an entire day, under a leaden sky and in heat like that of a furnace. For Tenn this meaningless activity was a wonderfully exciting game. Every hole yielded new and intoxicating smells. Whenever Friday paused to mop his forehead with his forearm Tenn dashed to the latest hole, burrowed into it with his nose, breathing like a grampus, and rapturously did his share of the digging, scattering the earth between his hind legs. Then he galloped round and round, barking and whining, and returned to intoxicate himself again in the trough where marl or dark humus mingled with the sap of cut roots, as death mingles with life when one has attained a certain depth.

To say that Friday gave no sign of resenting his idiotic employment is not enough. I have seldom seen him work with such goodwill. He did so, indeed, with an especial ardour which seems to refute the two alternative theories whereby I sought to account for him – either that he is utterly dull-witted, or that he believes me to be mad. I have to look elsewhere, and I find myself wondering whether Tenn's impassioned dance round those wounds gratuitously inflicted on the body of Speranza may not provide the clue; and whether, in seeking merely to humiliate Friday, I have not committed the unpardonable stupidity of revealing to him the secret of the pink combe.

It happened one night that Robinson could not sleep. A pool of moonlight shone on the floor of the Residence. An owl called in the darkness, and he seemed to hear the very earth groan with a plaint of love deprived. His mattress of dried grass felt incongruously soft and unreal. He lay for a while thinking of Tenn's mad, erotic dance round that open furrow, the body offered after being violated by Friday's spade. It was a long time since he had visited the combe. His daughters, the mandrakes, must have grown big by now! He sat up with his feet in the moonlight and smelt the scent of sap rising in his big body, white as a root. He rose silently, stepped over the entwined bodies of Friday and Tenn, and set out for the copse of gum-trees and sandalwood.

Chapter 8

When he entered the Residence, Friday saw at once that the water-clock had stopped. There was still water in the glass jar, but the hole had been plugged, and the level stood at three o'clock in the morning. It caused Friday no astonishment to find Robinson gone. To his mind the stopping of the clock quite naturally implied the absence of the Governor. Accustomed to take things as they came, he did not ask himself where Robinson was, or if he would come back, or even if he was still alive. Nor did he think of going to look for him. He was wholly absorbed in the contemplation of the familiar objects around him, which the stopping of the clock and Robinson's departure presented in an entirely new aspect. He was now his own master and master of the island. As though in confirmation of the new dignity conferred upon him, Tenn got lazily to his feet and came and stood in front of him, gazing up at him with nut-brown eyes. Tenn was not as young as he had been, and his round, barrel-like body, his over-short legs, his watery eyes and faded shaggy coat all bore witness to the ravages of age at the end of a well-spent dog's life. But he, too, seemed conscious of the novelty of the situation, and he waited for his friend to decide what they would do.

What to do? There could be no question of going on with the watering of the plot of rape and sorrel, rendered necessary by the drought, or with the building of a look-out post in the topmost branches of the giant cedar, since these things called for orders which must remain in abeyance until Robinson's return. Friday's gaze came to rest on a chest under the table, which was carefully closed but not locked, so that he had been able to inspect its contents. He dragged it out and, tilting it on end, lifted it on to his shoulder. Thus he left the Residence, followed by Tenn.

In the north-western part of the island, where the grass grew sparse as the meadowland merged into the sand-dunes, a cluster of weird, vaguely human shapes occupied the cactus garden which Robinson had established there. He had had misgivings about wasting so much time on an unproductive task, but they were plants that needed almost no attention; he had simply had to transplant the more interesting speci-mens, which were to be found all over the island, to the place that suited them best. He had done so in memory of his father, whose one passion, apart from his wife and children, had been for the tropical plants which he cultivated in a small conservatory. Robinson as a small boy had written their Latin names on wooden tablets stuck in the earth of their flowerpots, and these, by a trick of memory, he had subsequently recalled.

The chest hurt Friday's shoulder, and he let it fall to the ground. The lid burst open, and a wonderful confusion of rich clothes and jewels was spilled at the feet of the cacti. At last Friday was able to indulge his fancy in the use of these treasures, the sight of which enchanted him, although under Robinson's dispensation they had been merely the appurtenances of ceremony and discomfort. It was not his own body that he wished to adorn, since to him all clothing was an encumbrance, but the mysterious plants with their bloated green flesh and arresting gestures, which seemed to him more suited than any human form to display the splen-dour of the materials.

He first spread out the garments on the ground, that he might the better admire them. He found some flat stones, and on these he arranged the gems and precious metals as though

9

in a jeweller's shop-window. Then he spent some time going from one cactus to another, noting their shape and testing the firmness of their flesh with his fingers. They were a strange assortment of vegetable mannequins shaped like candelabra, like unearthly beasts, like humans with heavy heads, intertwined limbs and venomous-fingered hands adorned with pointed stars. Their surface was sometimes moist and pulpy, sometimes hard and rubbery, sometimes like green, open wounds exuding a smell of rotting flesh. At length Friday picked up a cloak of black watered silk and spread it with a flourish over the broad shoulders of a *Cereus pruinosus*. Then he draped a coquettish flounce over the swollen buttocks of a *Crassula falcata*. A lace handkerchief served as a garland for the spiky phallus of a *Stapelia variegata,* and he put a pair of gauze mittens on the small, downy fingers of a *Crassula lycopodiodes*. A brocade cap fitted admirably on the woolly head of a *Cephalocereus senilis.* Friday busied himself in this fashion for some time, wholly absorbed in his task, draping and re-arranging, standing back to judge the effect, and now and then undressing one cactus in order to clothe another. Finally he rounded off the composition with the jewellery, arranging bracelets, necklets, rings, buckles, crosses and diadems with equal care and discernment. But having completed it he spent no time in contemplating the pageant of lords and ladies and extravagant monsters he had caused to rise out of the sand. He had nothing more to do in that place and so he left it, with Tenn still at his heels.

He crossed the sand-dunes, listening with interest to the sort of earthy murmur set up by his feet. He paused and turning to the dog tried to imitate the sound, growling with his mouth closed. But Tenn was not amused, he was finding it difficult enough to plough his way over the soft sand, and at this added noise his hackles rose. The ground grew firm again as they came to the foreshore, which was largely uncovered by the ebb. Standing upright with his head flung back in the splendid light of the morning, Friday marched rejoicing over the great, flawless arena, drunk with youth and alacrity in that boundless space where every movement was possible and nothing met the gaze. He picked up an egg-shaped pebble and balanced it on his open palm. It was a composite in which crystals of pink feldspar were mingled with vitreous quartz flecked with mica, crude but unequivocal, and he liked it better than the jewels he had left on the cacti. Its curved surface touched his palm at only one point, making with it a pure and simple geometrical pattern. A wave ran up the beach, over the shining surface of wet sand dotted with small jellyfish, and washed round his ankles. Friday dropped the egg-shaped pebble and picked up another that was round and flat, a small opalescent disc splashed with mauve. He tossed it in his hand. If only he could fly! If he could turn himself into a butterfly! And the thought of making the stone fly suddenly delighted his Ariel-soul. He sent it skimming over the water, and it bounced seven times before sinking without a splash. But this was a game that Tenn knew. He plunged in after it, swimming with head raised and nose pointing to the horizon, dived and came back on the crest of a wave, to drop it at Friday's feet.

They walked eastward for a time and, after passing the dunes, turned towards the south. Friday picked up random objects, starfish, scraps of wood, shells, cuttle-bones, tufts of seaweed, and cast them from him, turning them into prey for Tenn, who ran barking after them. Then they came to the rice-paddy.

The reservoir was dry, and the level of water in the paddy was steadily falling. It needed to be kept under water for a month if the plants were to achieve their full growth, and Robinson's anxiety had increased every time he paid it a visit of inspection.

Friday still had a mauve pebble in his hand. He now

skimmed it over the paddy, counting the number of its bounces on the oily surface of the water. It bounced nine times, and Tenn at once leapt off the bank in pursuit of it. His initial impetus carried him a dozen yards, but then he came to a stop. The water was too shallow for him to swim, and he was engulfed in thick mud. He turned and tried to return to Friday, but although with a first effort he wrenched himself clear of the mud, he sank back into it, convulsively struggling. It was clear that he would drown if he were not rescued. Friday paused for an instant, gazing at the treacherous, unclean patch of water. Then, seeing what must be done, he ran to the outlet-sluice and passing a stick through the tap hole in the stem of the gate, began laboriously to heave it up, supporting himself by the uprights. As the gate slowly rose, creaking in its grooves, the carpet of slime covering the paddy began to shrink and the water drained away. A few minutes later Tenn got back to dry land, a solid mass of mud but safe and sound.

Leaving him to clean himself up, Friday went dancing towards the forest. The thought that the rice-crop was ruined had not occurred to him.

To Friday the stopping of the clock and the absence of Robinson had been two aspects of a single event, a break in the established order. To Robinson, Friday's disappearance, the dressing of the cacti and the drying out of the rice-paddy all pointed to the inadequacy and perhaps total failure of his attempts to domesticate the Araucanian. It was rare, in any case, for Friday to do anything of his own accord that did not displease Robinson. He could only escape rebuke by meticulously following instructions, or by doing nothing. Robinson had been obliged to recognize that beneath the show of submissiveness Friday possessed a mind of his own, and that what came out of it was profoundly shocking and subversive of discipline on the island.

He resolved at first to ignore Friday's disappearance; but after two days had passed, yielding to a complex feeling of disquiet mingled with curiosity, vague remorse and sympathy for Tenn, who was evidently distressed by the boy's absence, he went in search of him. During a whole morning he and Tenn combed the part of the forest into which Friday's tracks vanished. Here and there they discovered signs of his passing, and finally Robinson was forced to conclude that, in defiance of himself, Friday was hiding somewhere in that part of the island, living a life of outlawry and diverting himself with games which baffled Robinson. Wooden masks, a blowpipe, a hammock of lianas in which lay a figure made of raffia, plumed headdresses, snake-skins, the dead bodies of birds — all these were tokens of a secret world to which Robinson possessed no key. But his mystification reached its height some days later when he came to a stream bordered with small trees not unlike willows. These shrubs had all been uprooted and replanted upside down, with their topmost branches in the earth and their roots in the air. But what lent an air of fantasy to the extraordinary sight was the fact that the plants seemed to have adapted themselves to this strange mishandling. Shoots were beginning to appear on the roots, which suggested that the buried branches had turned themselves into roots and the sap was flowing in the opposite direction. Robinson could not tear himself away from his study of the phenomenon. That Friday should have had the idea and carried it out was disturbing enough in itself. But the shrubs had accepted it, Speranza herself had apparently acquiesced in the extravagance! In this case at least Friday's whimsical imagination had produced a result which, trivial though it was, had positive aspects and was not purely destructive. Robinson was still brooding over it on his way back from the stream when Tenn came to an abrupt stop at a thick clump of magnolia trees entwined with ivy, and after pointing with his body rigid, moved cautiously forward. He stopped again, sniffing at one of the trunks. And suddenly the tree-trunk stirred, while Friday's laugh rang out. Using the juice of some plant he had painted ivy-leaves on his naked body, their coils running up his thighs and round his torso. Thus transformed into a human plant, and squealing with demented laughter, he executed a wild dance round Robinson before dashing off to the seashore to wash himself. Robinson, silently watching, saw him vanish, still dancing, into the shade of the mangroves.

The moon that night shone dazzlingly down on the forest from a cloudless sky. Robinson closed the Residence, and leaving Friday and Tenn to look after each other, went along the sylvan corridor pierced with beams of silver light. Perhaps because they were hypnotized by the brilliance of the light, the small creatures whose rustlings generally filled the undergrowth were sunk in a solemn quiet. As he drew near the pink combe, Robinson felt the stress of his daily preoccupations loosen its hold on him and he was filled with marital tenderness.

Friday was causing him more and more concern. Not merely did he fail to fit harmoniously into the system, but, an alien presence, he even threatened to destroy it. Such destructive blunders as his draining of the rice-paddy might be condoned on the grounds of his youth and ignorance; but, with every appearance of good-will, he was proving himself utterly unreceptive to principles of order and organization, planning and husbandry. He makes more work than the work he does, Robinson reflected sadly, although with a suspicion that he might be slightly exaggerating. Moreover, the primitive instinct which enabled Friday to come to terms with, and one might even say, win the complicity of animals, while it was irritating in the case of Tenn, was nothing less than disastrous in its effect on the lower orders – goats, rabbits, even fish. There seemed to be no way of getting it into that thick, black skull that the livestock was selected, rounded up and fed for use as nourishment, and not for the sake of company, or to play at games of hunting and fishing. To Friday it was unthinkable that one should kill an animal except after a chase or a struggle which gave it a chance of survival – a dangerously romantic concept! Nor could he understand that there were harmful species which had to be fought to the death: he had even made pets of a pair of rats, which he encouraged to increase and multiply! Order was a fragile victory, painfully gained over the natural savagery of the island, and the blows dealt it by the Araucanian were doing it greater harm. Robinson could not permit himself the luxury of harbouring an element of misrule which threatened to bring down the edifice it had taken him years to build. But what was he to do?

Reaching the edge of the forest he paused for a moment, held spellbound by the beauty and tranquillity of the moon-lit scene. The meadow-land drifted away into shadow like a silken cloak fluttering here and there in the faint breeze. From beyond it, where the dense cluster of reeds stood stiffly upright like the raised lances of an army, there came the thin croaking of a tree-frog. A white owl that almost brushed him with its wing came to rest on a cypress, turning towards him its startled, dreamlike face. A breath of perfume told him that he was drawing near to the pink combe, whose soft ridges the moonlight threw into sharp relief. The mandrakes were now so numerous that the aspect of the place was changed. Robinson sat with his back against a hummock of sand and reached out a hand to the broad, purple-tinted leaves with their jagged edges, for whose growth on the island he was responsible. His fingers encountered the rounded shape of one of their brown fruits, which had a heavy, foetid smell, not easily forgotten. His daughters were there, the blessing of his union with Speranza, spreading their lace-edged petticoats over the dark grass, and he knew that if he pulled one out of the earth it would be to disclose the white, plump legs of her vegetable form. He lay down in a furrow which was somewhat rough but deep enough to enclose him and abandoned himself to the sensual torpor, rising from the earth, that penetrated his loins, while he pressed the warm, musky flesh of a mandrake blossom to his lips. He knew each one of those flowers from having counted their blue, violet, white and purple calices. But suddenly he started. The blossom in his hand was *striped*. It was white with dark markings. He shook himself into bewildered wakefulness. This particular plant had not been in flower two days before, when he had visited the combe by daylight, or he would have been struck by the new variant. In any case, he kept a meticulous chart of his seedings, and he would consult it when he got back to the Residence. But he was positive already that he had never before lain in the place where the striped mandrake was now in bloom.

He stood up. The charm was broken, all the blessing of that radiant night dispelled. A suspicion that was still vague was forming in his mind, to be turned at once into anger against Friday. The secret life, the bushes planted upside down, the strange disguise – even the dressed cacti and Tenn's dance over Speranza's wounds – were not these all clues to the mystery of the new mandrakes?

Journal

I returned to the Residence in a state of extreme agitation. My first impulse was, of course, to awaken the rogue, beat him until he confessed and then to beat him again for the crimes he confessed to. But I have learned never to act in anger. Anger impels us to action, but the action is always bad. I forced myself instead to stand erect at the lectern with my heels pressed together and read a passage taken at random from the Bible. It cost me a hard struggle, with my fury leaping within me like a kid pegged down with a too-short cord. At length calm returned to me as the majestic and bitter words from the *Book of Ecclesiastes* resounded from my lips. O, Book of Books, how many hours of serenity do I not owe to you! To read the Bible is to be raised to a mountain-peak whence I can encompass at a glance the whole island and the immensity of waters surrounding it. With all pettiness swept away my soul can spread its wings and soar, knowing only sublime and eternal things. The lofty pessimism of King Solomon was well fitted to appease the anger in my heart. It pleased me to read that there is no new thing under the sun, that all is vexation and vanity of spirit, that there is no remembrance of the wise more than of the fool, that it is vain to build and labour, to sow and reap, since all things turn to dust. It was as though the Sage of Sages were humouring my splenetic mood to prepare me for the one truth that was applicable in my case, which might indeed have lain in waiting through the ages for this moment. And when I came to them, the lines smote me like a corrective blow on the cheek.

Two are better than one; because they have a good reward for their labour.

For if they fall, the one will lift up his fellow: but woe to him that is alone when he falleth; for he hath not another to help him up.

Again, if two lie together, then they have heat: but how can one be warm alone?

And if one prevail against him, two shall withstand him; and a threefold cord is not quickly broken.

I read and re-read those words and was still repeating them when I retired to my couch. For the first time I asked myself if I had not sinned gravely against Charity in seeking by every means to compel Friday to submit to the laws of the cultivated island, since in doing so I proclaimed my preference, over my coloured brother, for the earth shaped by my own hands. Truly an ancient dilemma, the source of many a conflict and countless crimes.

Robinson therefore resolved to think no more about the striped mandrakes, and was assisted in his resolution by the urgent necessity for terracing and rebuilding after a series of torrential rains, which brought him and Friday closer together. The months passed in an alternation of stormy disagreements and tacit reconciliations. Although at times Robinson was profoundly shocked by his companion's doings, he concealed his vexation and later sought to excuse him when he sat down to write his journal. This happened in the matter of the turtle-shell shield.

Friday had been absent that morning for some hours when Robinson noticed a column of smoke rising above the trees from the direction of the beach. The lighting of fires on the island was not expressly forbidden, but the law required that due notice should be given, specifying the time and place, so that they might not be attributed to a new landing of the Araucanians. If Friday had neglected this precaution it could only be for reasons of his own; in other words, because he was intent on doing something which would incur his master's displeasure.

Closing his Bible with a sigh, Robinson whistled to Tenn and went down to the beach.

At first he could not understand what Friday was up to. He had rolled a large turtle on to its back on a heap of glowing cinders. The creature was by no means dead. Its legs were frantically waving, and Robinson thought he heard a hoarse, coughing sound which must be its cry of agony. To torture an animal in this fashion was abominable. Friday must be possessed by a devil! Robinson began to understand what he was doing when he saw that the shell was gradually losing its concave shape under the influence of the heat, while Friday was hard at work cutting the ligaments that attached it to the turtle's body. The shell was still not quite flat, more like a slightly curved tray, when the animal succeeded in rolling out of it and getting to its feet. Its back was a pulp, a hideous red and green distension like a bag bulging with blood and pus. With a nightmare speed, moving as fast as

Tenn who ran barking behind it, it made for the water and plunged into the waves. 'Stupid,' said Friday calmly. 'The crabs soon eat it.' He was now scouring the inside of the flattened shell with sand. 'No arrow pierce this shield,' he explained to Robinson. 'Even a heavy bolas not break it.'

Journal

It is a part of our English nature to show more mercy to animals than we do to men, an attitude of mind which is perhaps open to discussion. The fact remains that nothing has so set me apart from Friday as that unspeakable torture of an animal. Yet his is not a simple case and it raises many questions.

I thought at first that he had an affection for my animals. But his instant and seemingly instinctive understanding with them – with Tenn, with the goats, even with the rats and vultures – has nothing in common with my own sentimental fondness for the lower orders of creation. It would seem indeed that his relationship to animals is itself more animal than human. He is on their level. He never seeks to improve their lot, still less to make himself loved by them. He treats them with a casual indifference, a cruelty, that revolts me but does not seem at all to diminish their friendliness for him. The bond of complicity, as it seems, goes deeper than any torment he may inflict on them. When it dawned upon me that he would not hesitate, in case of need, to cut Tenn's throat and eat him, and that the dog's obscure awareness of this did not in any way affect its preference for him over myself, I had a feeling of anger mingled with jealousy at so much stupidity and blindness to self-interest. But I have realized that we may only compare like with like, and that Friday's relationship with animals is wholly different from my own. They accept him as one of themselves. He owes them nothing and may in innocence exercise over them all the rights conferred upon him by his superior strength and cunning. I seek to persuade myself that in doing so he makes manifest the animal in himself.

Not long after this Friday became interested in a fledgling vulture which he rescued after its mother had turned it out of the nest for reasons of her own. Its ugliness might have justified the expulsion had it not been typical of the species. The featherless, misshapen, lurching little creature greeted all-comers with a gaping beak at the end of a naked neck, above it two enormous closed lids, violet-tinted, that were like boils swollen with matter.

Friday at first thrust scraps of fresh meat into its mouth and these were gulped down with an eagerness which suggested that they would have been swallowed no less readily if they had been pebbles. But a day or two later the little creature fell sick. It grew lethargic and spent most of the time sleeping. When Friday felt its crop he found it hard and distended with food, although some hours had elapsed since its last meal. In a word, it showed symptoms of acute and possibly fatal indigestion.

Accordingly Friday put some goat's entrails to cook in the sun, where they lay in a cloud of flies, giving off a stench that turned Robinson's stomach but seemed to revive the vulture's appetite. And when a quantity of small white grubs appeared on the nauseous, half-liquid mess Friday performed an operation which Robinson was never to forget. Scraping at some of it with a shell he put it in his mouth, grubs and all, and sat methodically chewing while he gazed absently about him. Then, bending over his foster-child's beak, which was held out to him like a blind man's begging-bowl, he let the unspeakable white pap dribble into it, while the little creature quivered with delight.

'Living worms too fresh,' he explained to Robinson. 'Little bird ill, so chew-chew. Always chew for little birds.'

Robinson fled with his stomach heaving, but Friday's devotion and calm logic greatly impressed him. For the first time he questioned his white man's sensibilities, the queasy fastidiousness, wondering if this were a last rare token of civilization or no more than a dead weight which he must resolve to shed if he were to embark upon a new way of life.

But there were times when the Governor, the General and the Pastor gained the upper hand in Robinson. His mind dwelt on the ravages caused by Friday in the meticulous ordering of the island, the ruined crops, the wasted stores and scattered herds; the vermin that multiplied and prospered, the tools that were broken or mislaid. All this might have been endurable had it not been for the *spirit* manifested by Friday, the tricks and devices, the diabolical or impish notions that entered his head, setting up a confusion by which Robinson was himself infected. And the sum of his grievances was contained in the striped mandrake, the thought of which haunted him and kept him awake at night.

It was in one of his fits of rage that he made himself a whip out of plaited strips of goat-hide. He did so with a feeling of secret shame, dismayed by the growth of hatred in his heart. Not merely was Friday playing havoc with Speranza, he was poisoning his master's soul! Indeed, Robinson was beginning to have thoughts which he dared not avow, all centred on the theme of Friday's death, natural, accidental or contrived.

Things had reached this pass when one morning a fateful presentiment drew his footsteps to the copse of gum-trees and sandalwood. A splash of brilliant colour flew out of a clump of thuya and rose circling into the air, a big and splendid butterfly with wings of black velvet and gold. The whiplash whistled and cracked and the living flower fluttered in fragments to the earth. This was another thing that Robinson would not have done a few months earlier . . . It was true that the fire he felt blazing within him seemed to him more exalted, more pure in its essence, than any simple human passion. As in all things affecting his relations with Speranza, there was something cosmic in his fury. He did not see himself in commonplace terms, as a plain man enraged, but as a primitive force issued from the bowels of the earth to sweep all things away with a searing breath. A volcano. A volcano bursting through Speranza's surface in the deep-buried fury of rock and alluvial soil. Moreover, for some time past, whenever he had opened the Bible it was to hear the thundering of Jehovah.

Behold, the name of the Lord cometh from far, burning with his anger, and the burden thereof is heavy: his lips are full of indignation, and his tongue is a devouring fire:

And his breath, as an overflowing stream, shall reach to the midst of the neck, to sift the nations with the sieve of vanity: and there shall be a bridle in the jaws of the people, causing them to err.

In reading those verses aloud Robinson could not subdue the bellowing of his own voice, which both eased and inflamed him. He seemed to see himself standing on the topmost pinnacle of the island, terrible and sublime.

And the Lord shall cause his glorious voice to be heard, and shall shew the lighting down of his arm, with the indignation of his anger, and with the flame of a devouring fire, with scattering, and tempest, and hailstones.   Isaiah, XXX

The whip cracked again, directed at the form of a vulture soaring lazily high above, far beyond Robinson's reach, but in his fog of exaltation he saw it fall to the ground at his feet, broken and quivering, and he burst into savage laughter.

But in the heart of this desert of despair there was yet a stream of consolation. The pink combe with its welcoming folds, its lascivious undulations, was still there, cool and healing in the sweetness of its scented skin. Robinson went more quickly. In a few moments he would be able to stretch himself on that feminine earth, lie on his back with his arms crossed, and it would seem to him that he was plunging into an abyss of blue, bearing all Speranza on his back as Atlas did the terrestrial globe. Then, with strength renewed by contact with that primal source, he would turn to press his loins to the huge, warm female body, to furrow it with a plough of flesh.

142

He paused at the edge of the forest, with the breasts and groins of the combe spread out before him. The handsbreadth leaves of the mandrakes, his daughters, seemed to wave in welcome, and a warmth stirred in his loins and sweet moisture filled his mouth. Singing to Tenn to wait for him under the trees, he hurried as though borne on wings to his wedded couch. There was a marshy patch enclosing a small, still pool with a scattering of pale sand at its edges overgrown with soft grass. This was where he would today make love. He knew that grassy nook already, and the violet-tinted gold of mandrake blossoms already shone there.

And there he saw two small black buttocks half-buried in the leaves and hard at work, rising and falling, swelling and contracting, like a swift-gathering and receding tide. Robinson stood like a sleepwalker harshly awakened from a dream of love. He stood thunderstruck, contemplating the infamy that was taking place beneath his eyes, the sullying, the outraging of Speranza by a Negro! The striped mandrakes would be appearing here, too, in a few weeks' time! And he had left his whip at the edge of the forest with Tenn! He kicked Friday to his feet, stretched him on the grass again with a blow of his fist and then fell upon him with all his white man's weight and strength. No thought now of lovemaking! He beat him with clenched fists like a man deaf and blind, deaf to the cries that issued from the boy's bleeding lips. He was possessed of a sacred fury. He was the Flood drowning human iniquity over the whole surface of the globe, the fire from Heaven purging Sodom and Gomorrah, the Seven Plagues chastising Pharoah for his hardness of heart. But at length a few words gasped out by Friday penetrated this blanket of Godlike wrath – 'Master, don't kill me!' Robinson's grazed fist fell once more, but half-heartedly, and then was stayed in a painful effort of reflection. It dawned upon him that he was enacting another, long familiar scene, a scene of brother beating brother to death at the side of a ditch, the first murder in recorded history, the murder of all murders. Who was he, then? Was he the avenging son of Jehovah, or was he marked with the brand of Cain? He got to his feet and turned and ran to cleanse himself in the source of all wisdom . . .

Again he stood at the lectern, heels together and hands joined, awaiting the guidance of the Holy Spirit. He wanted to raise the level of his anger, render it more lofty and more pure. Opening the Bible at random he came upon the *Book of Hosea*. The words of the prophet sprang at him, black upon the white page, as lightning precedes thunder, before they resounded from his lips. And it was to his daughters, the mandrakes, that he was speaking, warning them against their mother, the adulterous earth:

Plead with your mother, plead: for she is not my wife, neither am I her husband: let her therefore put away her whoredoms out of her sight, and her adulteries from between her breasts;

Lest I strip her naked, and set her as in the day that she was born, and make her as a wilderness, and set her like a dry land, and slay her with thirst.

The Book of Books had spoken, and it was Speranza who stood condemned! This was not what Robinson had looked for. He had wanted to read in letters of fire the condemnation of the unworthy servant, that seducer and violator. He closed the Book and opened it again at random. Now it was *Jeremiah* who spoke, and he spoke of the striped mandrakes in the image of the strange vine:

For of old time I have broken thy yoke, and burst thy bands; and thou saidst, I will not transgress; when upon every high hill and under every green tree thou wanderest, playing the harlot.

Yet I had planted thee a noble vine, wholly a right seed: how then art thou turned into the degenerate plant of a strange vine unto me?

For though thou wash thee with nitre, and take thee much soap, yet thine iniquity is marked before me, saith the Lord God.

But if Speranza had seduced Friday, was that to say that the boy was wholly innocent and blameless? With his outraged heart in rebellion against this verdict that condemned Speranza, and her alone, Robinson again closed and opened his Bible. He opened it at the *Book of Genesis*, and read aloud as follows:

And it came to pass after these things, that his master's wife cast her eyes upon Joseph; and she said, Lie with me.

But he refused, and said unto his master's wife, Behold, my master wotteth not what is with me in the house, and he hath committed all that he hath to my hand;

There is none greater in this house than I; neither hath he kept back any thing from me but thee, because thou art his wife; how then can I do this great wickedness, and sin against God?

And it came to pass, as she spake to Joseph day by day, that he hearkened not unto her, to lie by her, or to be with her.

And it came to pass about this time, that Joseph went into the house to do his business; and there was none of the men of the house there within.

And she caught him by his garment, saying, Lie with me: and he left his garment in her hand, and fled, and got him out.

And it came to pass, when she saw that he had left his garment in her hand, and was fled forth,

That she called unto the men of her house, and spake unto them, saying, See, he hath brought in an Hebrew unto us to mock us; he came in unto me to lie with me, and I cried with a loud voice:

And it came to pass, when he heard that I lifted up my voice and cried, that he left his garment with me, and fled, and got him out.

10

And she laid up his garment by her, until his lord came home.

And she spake unto him according to these words, saying, The Hebrew servant, which thou hast brought unto us, came in unto me to mock me:

And it came to pass, as I lifted up my voice and cried, that he left his garment with me, and fled out.

And it came to pass, when his master heard the words of his wife, which she spake unto him, saying, After this manner did thy servant to me; that his wrath was kindled.

And Joseph's master took him, and put him into the prison, a place where the king's prisoners were bound: and he was there in the prison.

Robinson fell silent in dismay. He was sure that his eyes had not deceived him. He had beyond question surprised Friday in the act of fornication with the earth of Speranza. But he also knew that for a long time past he had needed to interpret external facts, however indisputable, as so many tokens of a deeper truth, still buried and in process of becoming. Friday planting his black seed in the earth of the pink combe, whether in a spirit of imitation or in sheer impudence, was an incidental happening, as much an anecdote as that tale of Joseph and Potiphar's wife. Robinson was becoming ever more conscious of the gap between the image of the island projected into his mind by his garbled recollections of human society, or his reading of the Bible, and the inhuman, primitive and uncompromising world whose truth he was timidly seeking. The truth that was in him, which had never deceived him, was warning him in veiled terms that the period of the island-wife – following the period of the island-mother, which itself had followed that of the cultivated island – was now at an end, and that some new development was approaching, utterly strange and unpredictable.

Leaving the lectern, he moved quietly and thoughtfully

to stand in the doorway of the Residence. Here he had a movement of recoil, and his anger flared up again, when at his left hand he saw Friday squatted motionless on his heels with his back against the wall of the hut, gazing into space. The boy was capable of remaining like this for hours, in a posture which he himself could not sustain for more than a few minutes without getting severe cramp in his legs. A prey to conflicting emotions, Robinson finally took it upon himself to sit down beside Friday, to commune with him in the deep hush of silent expectation that now enveloped Speranza and its inhabitants.

The sun shone down in all-powerful majesty out of a cloudless sky, casting its golden weight on the sea stretched beneath it in total submission, on the dried and swooning island, on Robinson's buildings which at that moment were like so many temples consecrated to its splendour. The truth within him murmured to Robinson that perhaps one day the earthly reign of Speranza would be succeeded by a *solar* reign, but the thought was still so vague, so weak and difficult to grasp, that he could not long contemplate it and put it away for the time being, to let it ripen in his mind.

Turning his head, he studied Friday's face in profile. Its right side was covered with cuts and bruises, and there was a purple gaping gash over the high checkbone. As though he were observing him through a magnifying glass, Robinson considered the prognathous, slightly animal countenance, rendered more than usually stubborn and sulky at that moment by the boy's distress. And it was now that he became aware of something pure and sensitive gleaming amid the unsightly, mishandled flesh. He noted Friday's eye, beneath its long, curved lashes, seeing how the wonderfully smooth and limpid ball was incessantly wiped clean and refreshed by the beating of the lid. He noted the constant widening and shrinking of the pupil, in response to the scarcely perceptible variation of the light, as it regulated the message to be transmitted to the retina. Within the transparency of the iris was contained a tiny, intricate pattern like feathers of glass, a cultivated rose, infinitely precious and delicate. It was a beautiful thing, so finely contrived, so perfectly new and shining. How did it come about that this marvel should be part of a creature so coarse, so graceless and uncouth? And if he had only at this moment perceived its beauty, must he not in honesty ask himself whether Friday might not be the sum of other attributes no less admirable, which in his blindness he had failed to see?

Robinson turned the question over in his mind. For the first time he was clearly envisaging the possibility that within the crude and brutish half-caste who so exasperated him another Friday might be concealed – just as he had once suspected, before exploring the cave or discovering the combe, that another Speranza might be hidden beneath his cultivated island.

But this thought, too, was soon dismissed, and life resumed its arduous and monotonous course.

Life resumed its daily course, but now there was always something in Robinson which looked for a decisive event, something overwhelming, a radically new beginning which would reduce to nothingness all his past undertakings and future plans. The man he had been might protest at this, might continue doggedly to labour, reckoning the amount of next season's harvest, planning new crops of grasses and rare woods, even designing a water-mill to be built on one of the streams . . . But Robinson never went back to the pink combe.

Friday was troubled by no such problems. He had discovered the tobacco-jar, and he smoked Van Deyssel's pipe in secret. His punishment, if he were caught, would certainly be severe, for the tobacco was nearly all gone and Robinson allowed himself only one pipe every other month. It was an indulgence to which he looked forward long in advance, and he dreaded the day when it would come to an end. He went down one morning to inspect the fishing-lines he had laid out at low water the night before, which should now be uncovered by the ebb. Friday tucked the tobacco-jar under his arm and made for the cave. He got no pleasure out of smoking in the open air, but if he smoked in any of the buildings the smell would give him away. Robinson could smoke anywhere. For him all that mattered was the spluttering bowl, the earthly container of a small, subterranean sun, as it were a tamed, portable volcano which glowed peaceably under its ashes at the summons of his mouth. In that miniature retort the smouldering tobacco was transmuted into resins and tars whose scented essence agreeably titillated his nostrils. It was the possessed nuptial chamber, held in the hollow of his hand, of the earth and the sun.

For Friday, on the contrary, the delight of smoking lay wholly in the rising eddy of smoke, and the least draught robbed it of its charm. He needed to smoke in an absolutely sheltered place, and nowhere suited his airy pleasure better than the motionless air of the cave.

Using sacks and barrels he had made a sort of *chaise longue* for himself about a dozen yards from the entrance, and here he reclined, drawing deeply on the horn mouthpiece of the pipe, then allowing a thin stream of smoke to drift upwards from his lips, part and be sucked without loss into his nostrils. The smoke thus performed its major function: it pervaded and sensitized his lungs, bringing consciousness and a kind of luminosity to that concealed hollow in his chest which was the most aerial and spiritual part of himself. Finally he gently expelled the blue cloud that had inhabited it. Seen against the light coming from the entrance to the cave, the smoke spread like the tentacles of an octopus, rising in arabesques and slow, spreading coils that became ever more tenuous... Friday lay dreaming, and he was about to draw again on the pipe when he heard a distant sound of shouting and barking. Robinson had returned sooner than he expected, and he was calling to him in a voice that boded no good. Tenn gave a yelp as the whip cracked. Robinson's voice grew louder, more threatening, and then his figure appeared outlined in the mouth of the cave, striding with clenched fists and the whip whistling above his head. Friday jumped to his feet. What was he to do with the pipe? He flung it with all his strength into the depths of the cave, and then went bravely to meet his chastisement. Robinson must have noticed the removal of the tobacco-jar because he was beside himself with fury. He raised the whip . . . and it was at this moment that the forty barrels of powder exploded as one. A great burst of flame swept through the cave. In his last moment of consciousness Robinson felt himself lifted and hurled backwards, while he saw the mass of loose rock above the cave come tumbling down like a child's toy.

Chapter 9

When his eyes opened Robinson found a black face bent over him. Friday was lifting his head with one hand while he tried to get him to drink water from the cupped palm of the other. Robinson's mouth convulsively closed, and the water spilled over his beard and chest. Seeing him move, Friday stood up smiling, and a part of his scorched and blackened shirt, and his left trouser-leg, fell to the ground. He laughed and wriggled out of the rest of his shredded garments. Then, retrieving a piece of mirror from the debris of their home, he looked at himself in it, pulled a face, and offered it to Robinson, laughing again. Robinson's face was blackened and his red beard was singed, but there was no other sign of damage. He, too, stood up and stripped off the rags still clinging to him. He walked a few paces. It seemed that he was suffering from nothing more than a few bruises under the thick coating of dust and grime.

The Residence was burning like a torch. The crenellated wall of the fortress had collapsed into the moat. The office building, the Meeting House and the calendar-mast, being lighter, had been simply blown to bits. As Robinson and Friday stood contemplating the scene of devastation a mass of earth rose into the air some fifty yards away accompanied by a shattering explosion which again flung them to the ground. It must have been the charge of powder Robinson had buried outside the walls as a defence against invaders, with a fuse running to the fortress. Not until he was satisfied that all the powder was disposed of did Robinson pluck up courage to get to his feet again and review the disaster.

The goats, terrified by this second explosion, which was much closer to them, had broken down the fence of their enclosure and were now bolting in every direction. Within an hour they would have scattered all over the island and within a week they would have reverted to their natural state. Where the entrance to the cave had been there was now an avalanche of great boulders shaped like towers, pyramids, prisms and cylinders, a mountain of rubble dominated by a vertical spire of rock which must afford an admirable view over the island and the sea. The explosion, in short, had not been merely destructive; it was as though some architectural genius, operating at the point of extreme violence, had used it to indulge a fancy for baroque design.

Robinson gazed dumbly about him, and began mechanically to pick up the odds and ends that had been blown out of the cave before it collapsed. There were torn garments, a musket with a twisted barrel, fragments of earthenware, charred sacks and split baskets. He examined each object in turn before depositing it gently at the foot of the giant cedar. Friday followed his example, but without being very helpful. To preserve and repair was not in his nature, and he was more likely to complete the destruction of the things he handled. Robinson was too stunned to be angry, and he made no protest even when he saw the boy throw away several handfuls of wheat that had remained in the bottom of a jar. It was growing dark, and they had found one object that was still intact, namely the spyglass, when they came upon the body of Tenn stretched under a tree. Friday left and probed it for a long time. No bones were broken and indeed it bore no sign of injury, but the old dog was undoubtedly dead. Poor faithful Tenn – perhaps he had simply died of fright. They resolved to bury him in the morning. The wind was getting up. They went together to wash themselves in the sea, and then made a meal of wild bananas – and Robinson recalled that these were the first things he had eaten on the island. Not knowing where else to sleep they lay down amid their shattered belongings under the cedar. The sky was clear, but a strong north-westerly breeze was whipping the tops of the trees. The heavy branches of the cedar, however, were scarcely affected by this commotion, and Robinson lay on his back gazing up at their tranquil, lacy pattern outlined as though with Chinese ink against a background of stars.

It seemed, then, that Friday had triumphed at last over the state of affairs he so detested! He had not, of course, deliberately caused the disaster. Robinson well knew that calculations of that sort were quite out of keeping with his character. Friday was not a rational being, performing deliberate, considered acts, but rather a force of nature from which actions proceeded, and their consequences bore a kind of resemblance to him, in the way that children resemble their mother. Nothing, it seemed, could blunt his natural spontaneity, and Robinson realized that in this profound matter his influence over the boy was nil. Unwittingly but inexorably Friday had paved the way for, and finally achieved, the cataclysm that must herald the coming of a new era; and as for the nature of this new era, clearly it was in the nature of Friday himself that Robinson must look for it. He was still too much the prisoner of the man he had been to be able to predict what form it would take. The gulf that separated him from Friday far exceeded, even though it encompassed, the day-to-day antagonisms between the methodical, parsimonious, melancholy-minded Englishman and the laughing, exuberant, uninhibited native of a warmer clime. Friday was instinctively repelled by the sober order which Robinson had imposed on the island and which had enabled him to survive. It seemed indeed that he belonged to some quite other order, wholly opposed to that order of earth and husbandry, on which he could only have a disrupting effect if the effort were made to confine him within it.

The explosion had still not quite destroyed the former man in Robinson: the thought occurred to him, as he looked at his sleeping companion, that he could very easily kill him – he deserved death a hundred times over! – and then methodically set about the rebuilding of his shattered world. That he did not do so was not due solely to his fear of solitude, or his instinctive recoil from the act of violence. The truth was that the cultivated island had begun to oppress him almost as much as it had Friday. In his heart he had longed for something of this kind to happen. And so, having released him from his earthly bonds, it was for Friday to show him the way to *something else*, substituting for a way of life he had found intolerable some other order appropriate to himself, which Robinson was now eager to discover. A new Robinson was sloughing off the skin of the old, prepared to accept the decay of his cultivated island and, at the heels of an unthinking guide, to enter upon an unknown road.

He had reached this point in his reflections when he felt a movement beneath his hand as it lay palm-down on the earth. He thought at first that it was some insect and explored the surface with his finger-tips. But it was the earth itself that was rising at that point. A field-mouse, perhaps, or a mole about to emerge from its digging; and Robinson smiled at the thought of the little creature's terror when it found itself trapped in a prison of flesh instead of reaching open air. The earth moved again and something did emerge, but it was something cold and hard that still remained anchored in the soil! A root! It seemed that to crown that day of terror the very roots were coming to life and thrusting their way out of the ground! In a mood to accept every miracle, Robinson continued to gaze up at the stars through the branches of the tree. He saw a group of stars slide suddenly to the right, vanishing behind a branch to reappear on its other side. There was a brief pause, and then came a hideous sound of creaking and rending. By now Friday had sprung to his feet and was tugging at Robinson's arm. They ran frantically with the ground heaving beneath them while the crest of the cedar swung slowly through the stars; and with a sound of thunder the great tree crashed down among the other trees, like a giant falling into long grass. Its roots, now exposed, held a hillock of earth embraced in their numberless, twisted arms. The crash was followed by an awe-inspiring silence. Its foundations undermined by the explosion, the tutelary genius of Speranza had after all not been able to resist the steady pressure of the night wind sweeping over the island, gustless though it was.

This latest blow to the earthly being of Speranza, following the destruction of the cave, broke the last bond uniting Robinson to the life he had hitherto lived. Henceforward he was a wanderer, footloose and timorous, in the sole company of Friday. He would never again let go the hand that had reached down to save him on the night the tree fell.

Friday's freedom, as Robinson discovered in the days that followed, was something more than a mere negation of the order that the explosion had destroyed. His experience during his early days on Speranza had made Robinson too familiar with the life of utter purposelessness, at the mercy of every whim and a prey to every frustration, for him not to realize that there was an underlying wholeness, an implicit principle, at the heart of Friday's way of life.

Friday never worked in any real sense of the word. Unconcerned with past or future, he lived wholly in the moment. He would lie for days on end in the hammock he had made for himself, slung between two pepper-trees, using a blow-pipe to bring down birds which perched in the branches above him, tricked by his immobility; and in the evening he would drop his bag at Robinson's feet with an offhand gesture which might have been that of a faithful retriever or, on the other hand, of a master so sure of his authority that he did not trouble to give orders. But the truth was that the relationship between them now extended beyond either of those poles. Robinson now observed Friday with a passionate interest in his every act and in the effect of his actions upon himself, where they were producing an astonishing metamorphosis.

The first thing to be affected was Robinson's appearance. He gave up shaving his skull and let his hair grow in tangled locks that grew daily more luxuriant. But on the other hand, he trimmed his beard, after its singeing by the explosion, and every day he scraped his cheeks with the blade of his clasp knife, painstakingly honed with a piece of the pumice-stone that was common on the island. This not only did away with the solemn, patriarchal air, the loftiness of God-the-Father, which had sustained him in his former dignity; it also made him look ten years younger. A glance in the mirror even told him that, by a perfectly explicable phenomenon of mimicry, there was now a perceptible resemblance between his face and that of his companion. For years he had been both Friday's master and his father. Now in a matter of days he had become his brother and he was not even sure of being the elder brother. His body was also changed. Having always held the tropical sun to be among the worst perils threatening an Englishman, particularly a fair-skinned, red-headed one, he had been at pains to protect himself against its rays, even to the carrying of his goatskin parasol. His periods of retreat in the cave, and later his intimacy with the earth, had endowed his skin with the delicate, milky whiteness of underground shoots and tubers. But now, encouraged by Friday, he went naked under the sun. He had done so timidly at first, shrinking and ugly, but gradually he unfolded. His skin turned copper-coloured; a new pride swelled his chest and muscles; a warmth flowed through his body from which, as it seemed to him, his soul derived a hitherto unsuspected sustenance. In a word he found that a body which is accepted and rejoiced in – even vaguely desired, in a kind of unconscious narcissism – is not only a better instrument for use in dealing with the external world, but also a sturdy and loyal companion.

In company with Friday he engaged in sports and pastimes which formerly he would have considered beneath him. For example, he was not content until he could walk on his hands as well as Friday. He could stand on them easily enough with his feet against a rock, but directly he attempted to move away he fell over, not because his arms lacked the strength to support him, but from lack of skill and balance. He steadfastly persevered, with a feeling that by acquiring a greater versatility in the use of his limbs he was making progress on the new road he sought to follow. He had visions of his body transformed into one large hand, his head, arms and legs its five fingers – legs capable of pointing like a forefinger, arms capable of serving as legs, the body capable of resting on any of its limbs like a hand poised on one finger or another.

Among Friday's rare employments was the making of bows and arrows, which he did with a meticulous care that was the more remarkable inasmuch as he seldom used them for hunting. After experimenting with various woods for the bows he discovered a kind of boxwood, which he reinforced with strips of goatshorn to increase its strength and resilience. But it was to the arrows that he gave particular attention, devoting hours to consideration of the weight and thickness of the shafts and the delicate balance between the tip and the 'flight'. Indeed, from the pains he took with the flights, experimenting with different kinds of feather and even with leaves, and from his manner of carving the bone tips, it was evident that he was less concerned with hitting a target than with producing a missile that would travel as far as possible.

When he drew his bow it was with a rapt expression, one of almost painful concentration, as he sought for the correct angle to ensure his arrow the most impressive trajectory; and having released it he would stand watching its flight with both arms upflung, in an attitude that was almost one of prayer. His face glowed with pleasure so long as it soared upwards, but something seemed to snap in him when, losing momentum, it turned on its downward course.

For a long time Robinson was puzzled by this passion, which Friday pursued to the point of exhaustion, for the seemingly aimless pastime of shooting arrows without any thought of a target; but he came to understand it better on a day when a stiff sea-breeze was driving breakers up the beach. Friday was experimenting with a new design of arrow having a particularly long and elaborate flight made of albatross quills. He shot one in the direction of the woods at an angle of forty-five degrees. The arrow rose to a height of some 150 feet; but then, instead of diving back to earth, it hesitated, levelled out and glided over the tree-tops out of their sight. Friday turned with a glowing face to Robinson.

'It'll fall among the trees,' Robinson said. 'You'll never find it again.'

'No, I not find it again,' said Friday. 'That one never fall.'

Being restored to their natural state, the goats ceased to live in the state of anarchy imposed on animals by domestication at the hands of men. They broke up into hierarchical flocks led by the strongest and wisest males. When danger threatened they clustered tightly together, generally on a high place, and those on the outside confronted the aggressor with lowered horns. Friday amused himself by challenging any male goat he could catch. He would seize them by the horns and throw them, and if he had to chase one he would celebrate his victory by tying a garland of creeper round its neck.

But one day he was himself overthrown by a particularly large and fierce male with huge, knotted horns starting like black flames out of its head. It knocked him backwards down a rocky slope, and he had to spend three days in his hammock recovering. During this time he talked of nothing but his return match with the animal, whom he christened Andoar, and for whom he seemed to have conceived a lively feeling of affection and esteem. Andoar could be detected at two arrow-flights' distance by his powerful smell; he never ran away when approached; he generally stayed apart from the herd; above all, he made no attempt to savage Friday after knocking him down, as any other he-goat would have done. While he thus sang Andoar's praises Friday was busy making him a special halter, stronger and more brightly coloured than the garlands he had made for the other males. When he again set out for the rocky place where Andoar lived, Robinson uttered a mild word of protest, not expecting it to be listened to. The stench which clung to Friday after these encounters was in itself a reason for protesting; but in any case they were dangerous, as his recent misadventure had shown. Friday took no notice. He was as lavish in the expenditure of strength and courage in any sport that pleased him as he was feckless and indolent in everyday matters. He had found in Andoar a worthy adversary, and he cheerfully accepted the risk of further injury, even of death.

He had no difficulty in coming up with him. The great male was standing like a rock amid a herd of females and kids which scattered at Friday's approach. They were left alone in a natural arena, bounded at its far end by a slope of rubble overgrown with cactus, and on one side by a precipice two hundred feet deep. Friday untied the halter, which he had twisted round his wrist, and waved it like a gauntlet at Andoar. The goat abruptly stopped grazing and looked up with a stalk of grass hanging from its lips. Then it seemed to grin and reared up on its hind legs; and thus walked several

paces towards Friday, waving its forefeet and nodding its
immense horns as though acknowledging the applause of a
crowd of spectators. This astonishing performance turned
Friday rigid with amazement. When it was within a few
yards of him the goat dropped its forefeet to the ground and
suddenly charged like a battering-ram – or a great arrow
with a flight of fur – with its head lowered and its horns
aimed at Friday's chest. Friday flung himself sideways a
fraction of a second too late. A musky smell filled his nostrils
while at the same instant a violent blow to his right shoulder
caused him to spin round. He fell heavily and lay motionless, knowing that if he got up too soon he would be in no
condition to dodge another charge. He lay on his back
gazing with half-closed eyes at a fragment of blue sky
framed by stems of dried grass; and presently he saw a
face looking down at him like that of a Jewish patriarch, with
green eyes sunk in shaggy hollows, a curly beard, a dark
muzzle with lips drawn back in a faunlike grin. At his
feeble movement a searing pain shot through Friday's
shoulder and he fainted. When he again opened his eyes
the sun was blazing into them and its heat was intolerable.
Raising himself on his left arm he struggled halfway to his
feet, dizzily staring at the rubble-slope from which the sun's
rays rebounded over the arena. Andoar was nowhere to be
seen. Friday stood shakily upright and he was about to leave
the place when he heard the sound of hooves on the stones
behind him. The sound was so close that he did not attempt
to turn and face it, but flung himself to the left, to fall on
his sound arm. The blow caught him on the left hip as he
was in the act of falling, causing him to stagger with his
arms flung wide. The goat, its charge broken, came to an
abrupt stop beside him, and Friday, swayed, lost his balance,
and fell limply like a puppet on to its back. In agony from
the pain in his shoulder he clung there, gripping the base
of the knotted horns, while he wound his legs round the

beast's flanks and dug his toes into its belly. Andoar executed a series of astonishing leaps in his efforts to rid himself of this burden of naked flesh. Despite its weight, he galloped several times round the arena without losing his foothold amid the rocks. Had he fallen, or deliberately rolled over, he would not have been able to get up again. Friday by now was in so much pain that he was afraid of again losing consciousness. The goat had to be stopped. His hands slipped down over the bony forehead until they covered the eyes. But still Andoar continued his frantic career. As though the obstacles he could no longer see no longer existed, he charged straight ahead. His hooves clattered on the flat stones leading to the precipice, and the two bodies, locked together, plunged over the edge,

Robinson had witnessed the end of the struggle through his spyglass from a point some distance away. He knew that part of the island well enough to know that the shelf overgrown with brambles on to which they must have fallen could be reached either by a roundabout path from the top of the escarpment or, more directly, by climbing a hundred feet or so up the sheer rock face of which it was a part. Obviously he must go by the shortest route, although the prospect of the hazardous climb terrified him. But it was not only the need to save Friday, if he were still living, that impelled him to undertake it. Greatly though his physical aptitudes had improved in recent months, he knew that among the flaws inherited from his former self he still retained his intense horror of heights. He felt that in facing and overcoming this weakness he would be making a notable advance in his new way of life.

Running fast over the rocky ground, then leaping from rock to rock in the way he had so often seen Friday do, Robinson quickly reached the point where, clinging with fingers and toes to tiny hand- and foot-holds, he had to hoist himself up the smooth face of the cliff, which overhung in places. His first, but suspect, reaction was one of immense relief at finding himself in close contact with the elemental earth. His hands and feet, his whole naked body, knew the body of the mountain, its ridges and its crevices. He explored the surface with a sense of nostalgic delight in which concern for his physical safety played only a part. This, as he well knew, was a return to the past which would be an act of shameful and morbid surrender were it not for the *other half* of his ordeal, the empty space at his back. There was earth and air, and between them, clinging to the rock like a trembling butterfly, was Robinson, painfully striving to effect his conversion from one to the other. Halfway up the cliff, at a place where a narrow ledge made it possible, he compelled himself to pause and turn to face the emptiness. A cold sweat started on his forehead, and his hands grew dangerously slippery. He shut his eyes to avoid seeing the boulders over which he had sprung a few minutes before, which now seemed to be reeling through the air. But then he opened them again, resolved to conquer his weakness, and it occurred to him as he did so to look up at the evening sky, flooded with the last rays of the sunset. A sense of comfort instantly restored some part of his faculties. He realized that vertigo is nothing but terrestrial magnetism acting upon the spirit of man, who is the creature of earth. The soul yearns for that foot-hold of clay or granite, slate or silica, whose distance at once terrifies and attracts it, since it harbours the peace of death. It is not the emptiness of space that induces vertigo, but the enticing fullness of the earthly depths. With his face turned to the sky Robinson felt that something stronger than the insidious appeal of those scattered gravestones might be found in the summons to flight of two albatrosses companionably soaring amid the pink-tinted clouds. He continued to climb, fortified in his soul and knowing better where his next steps would lead.

It was dusk when he came upon the dead body of Andoar in a clump of thorn growing on the rocky shelf. Bending over the great shattered carcass, he saw the coloured garland securely twined round its neck. A laugh sounded behind him, and there was Friday standing upright, bruised and scratched all over and with his right arm hanging limply, but otherwise unharmed.

'He died and saved me with his coat,' he said. 'The great goat is dead, but I shall make him fly.'

Friday recovered from his battering with the rapidity that always astonished Robinson. Except for his shoulder, which was bruised and wrenched but did not seem to have been broken, he was well enough next morning to return to the scene and start operations on the body of Andoar.

First he cut off the head, which he placed on an ant-heap. Then, making a long incision down the chest and abdomen, and cutting round the legs, he stripped the skin from the body and spread it on the ground. He then gutted the body, removing its forty feet of intestines, and after carefully washing these in a nearby stream, draped them over the branches of a tree, a strange, bluey-white adornment which speedily attracted a multitude of flies. Then he walked singing down to the beach with Andoar's heavy, greasy pelt rolled in a bundle under his sound arm. After cleaning and soaking it thoroughly in sea-water he proceeded, using an improvised scraper made of a shell tied to a stone, to remove all the hair from one side and all traces of flesh from the other. This took him several days, during which he refused Robinson's offers of help, saying that he reserved for him a simpler and nobler task, and one that was no less important.

The nature of the task was disclosed when he asked Robinson to urinate on the skin, which was stretched out over a shallow basin in the rocks at a place where the spring tide had left a thin covering of water that evaporated in a few hours. He asked Robinson to drink a great deal during the next few days and to relieve himself nowhere else, because it was necessary for the whole skin to be soaked in urine. Robinson noted that he made no contribution of his own, but he refrained from asking whether this was because he considered his own urine to be lacking in the necessary virtues, or because he recoiled from the kind of intimacy which the mingling of their waters would have signified. After the skin had macerated for eight days in what became a brine of ammonia, Friday took it up, rinsed it in the sea and then fixed it to a framework made of two bows kept at a steady tension, which served as a stretcher. Finally, he put it to dry for three days in the shade, and then polished it with pumice while it still retained a trace of moisture. The skin was now a large strip of ancient-seeming parchment which gave out a sonorous note when he rubbed it with a finger.

'Andoar shall fly, Andoar shall fly,' Friday repeated in great excitement, but without saying precisely what he intended to do.

The araucarias on the island were not numerous but their tapered, black silhouettes rose majestically above the shrubs growing in their shade. Friday had a particular affection for these trees, which were so much a feature of his own country that his people derived their name from it, and he spent entire days cradled in their branches. When he came down he would bring Robinson a handful of winged seeds containing an edible nut strongly spiced with a sharp, resinous smell. Robinson had always refused to follow him on these climbs, which he considered too reminiscent of the apes.

On this particular day, finding himself at the foot of the tallest of the trees and gazing up through its branches, he calculated that it must be at least 150 feet in height. The brightness of the morning, after several days' rain, heralded the return of fine weather. The forest was steaming like an animal, and the plash of invisible rivulets in the depths of the mossy undergrowth set up an unaccustomed rippling sound. Always observant of changes in himself, Robinson had noted during the past weeks that he now impatiently awaited the rising of the sun, and that the spreading of its first rays had for him the solemnity of a festival which, though it happened daily, each time brought with it a feeling of intense novelty.

Gripping the lowest branch of the araucaria, he hoisted himself on to it, first kneeling and then standing upright, with the half-formed thought that by climbing to the top he would witness the sunrise a few minutes earlier. He continued to climb, doing so without difficulty and with a growing sense of being the prisoner, and in some sort a part, of a vast and infinitely ramified structure flowing upward through the trunk with its reddish bark and spreading in countless large and lesser branches, twigs and shoots to reach the nerve-ends of leaves, triangular, pointed, scaly and rolled in spirals round the twigs. He was participating in the evident function of the tree, which is to embrace the air with its thousand branches, to caress it with its million fingers. As he went higher he became conscious of the swaying of the giant architectural complex through which the blowing of the wind sounded an organ-note. He was near the top when suddenly he emerged into open space. The trunk, probably struck by lightning, was split and stripped at this point over a length of six feet. Robinson lowered his eyes in an attempt to escape from vertigo. Beneath his feet the successive levels of branches seemed to spin giddily into terrifying depths. A nightmare of his childhood returned to him. He had resolved to climb to the top of the tower of York Minster. After a long climb up the narrow circular stairway built round a sculptured stone pillar he had emerged suddenly from that protective darkness into the light of day, surrounded by space that was rendered the more vertiginous by the distant prospect of the roofs of the town. He had had to come down like a wrapped parcel, with his jacket pulled over his head . . .

He shut his eyes and pressed his cheek against the trunk of the tree, the one solid thing that was left to him. The labouring of that living mast, with its great burden of branches weaving the wind, was to be heard as a deep resonance now and then intermingled with a sustained groan. He listened to these soothing sounds for a long time, and by degrees his terror left him. He dreamed. The tree became a great ship anchored to the earth and struggling under full sail to break away from its mooring. A warm touch fell upon his cheek and a red glow traversed his eyelids. He knew that the sun had risen, but still waited a little before opening his eyes. He was absorbed in the strange new happiness rising within him, the warmth that enveloped him. After the gloom of the dawn the untamed light shone in sovereignty to make all things fruitful. He half-opened his eyes, seeing particles of brilliance dart beneath his lids. A warm breath set the leaves stirring. The leaf is the lung of the tree which is itself a lung, and the wind is its breathing, Robinson thought. He pictured his own lungs growing outside himself like a blossoming of purple-tinted flesh, living polyparies of coral with pink membranes, sponges of human tissue . . . He would flaunt that intricate efflorescence, that bouquet of fleshly flowers, in the wide air while a tide of purple ecstasy flowed into his body on the stream of crimson blood . . .

Across the river a great bird shaped like a lozenge the colour of old gold was dancing in the breeze. Friday had kept his promise to make Andoar fly.

After tying together three strips of cane to form a cross with two parallel transverse pieces of unequal length Friday had cut notches at their ends round which he twined a length of tightly strung gut which encircled the whole. To this light but sturdy framework he had fixed Andoar's skin, trimming it with an overlap that was folded over the gut and stitched to secure it. The shoulders of the skin covered the upper end of the cross, with the tail hanging from the lower end in the shape of a clover. A loose sling ran from the ends of the central stem, and to this the kite-string was attached at a point carefully calculated to ensure that the kite would ride at the correct angle. Friday had worked from the first flush of dawn to put the finishing touches to his creation, while the gusting south-westerly breeze, the harbinger of fine weather, caused the great bird to jerk and quiver in his hands as though it were impatient to take the air; and he had uttered a cry of delight when, bent like a bow, it had soared upward from the beach with its loose parts flapping, trailing a tail of alternating black and white feathers.

When Robinson joined him he was lying on his back on the sand with his hands clasped behind his neck and the kite-string tied to his left ankle. Robinson lay beside him and for a long time they watched the flight of Andoar in the heavens as he battled with the tricks of the wind, diving to its sudden gusts, turning when it veered, sinking when it slackened and in a soaring bound regaining the height he had lost. Friday, intensely participating in every movement, presently got to his feet and with arms outspread mimicked Andoar's dance. He crouched in a huddle on the sand, then sprang in the air, flinging his left leg high; he turned and twisted, stood limply when the wind failed him, and bounded up again; and the string tied to his ankle was like a choreographic score controlling the dance, for Andoar, his faithful partner, responded to his movements with dips and twirls of his own.

In the afternoon they fished for sea-pike in the lagoon at the eastern end of the island. Andoar, on a string about 150 feet long, was attached to the stern of the canoe, and a loose string of the same length, ending in a spray of cobweb, was tied to him, so that it hung down and brushed the crest of the waves. Robinson paddled slowly into the wind, while Friday sat with his back to him watching the kite. When a pike rose to the bait, locking its pointed jaws of small sharp teeth upon it, the kite dipped and jerked like an angler's float to warn them of the catch. Robinson then turned the canoe round and Friday grabbed the line when they came up to it. The canoe was presently heaped with cylindrical, green-backed and silver-flanked bodies of sea-pike

Friday could not bring himself to haul Andoar down that night. He tied him to one of the pepper-trees between which his hammock was slung. Like a dog on the lead, Andoar passed the night at his master's feet, and he followed him about all the next day. But during the night the wind dropped completely, and Andoar had to be retrieved from the clump of magnolias into which he had gently subsided. After several unsuccessful efforts Friday gave up trying to get him into the air again. He seemed then to forget all about him, and passed the next week in idleness. Then, suddenly as it seemed, he remembered the goat's head, which was still on the ant-heap where he had left it.

The ants had done their work well. Nothing remained of flesh or skin or the long brown and white hairs of the goat's beard. The eye-sockets and the inside of the skull were meticulously clean, all muscles and ligaments so thoroughly disposed of that the lower jaw fell away when Friday touched it. He held it up at arm's length as though it were a trophy, the ivory cranium with its black ringed horns shaped like a lyre, a most noble heraldic mask. Finding the brightly coloured garland which he had tied round the goat's neck, he affixed it to the horns, round the ridge which formed a bony swelling at their base.

'Andoar shall sing,' he said mysteriously to Robinson who was watching him.

First he carved two sticks of sycamore of different lengths, and drilling a hole at either end of the longer of the two, he thrust it over the points of the horns so that it linked them together. The shorter stick was fixed, parallel with the first, halfway down the muzzle; and about as much above it, between the eye-sockets, Friday fixed a bridge of pine with a dozen small notches in its outer edge. Then he got down Andoar's entrails from the tree where they were still hanging, now dried to ribbons by the sun, and cut them into equal segments about three feet long.

Robinson, still not understanding, watched him as he might have observed the behaviour of some insect whose intricate proceedings were unfathomable to the human mind. During most of his life Friday did nothing, and it seemed that boredom never intruded to ruffle the placidity of his immense and childlike indolence. But then, seized with an idea like a butterfly-grub summoned by the breath of spring to engage in the complicated business of reproduction, he would jump to his feet and become wholly absorbed in activities whose purpose long remained mysterious, but which nearly always had something to do with the air and the sky. When this happened neither time nor effort counted with him, and there was no limit to his perseverance or his patience. So Robinson watched while, during the next few days, Friday secured the twelve strings of gut by means of pegs to the cross-pieces fixed to Andoar's horns and muzzle. He then proceeded to tune them, doing so with an instinctive musical sense, not running up the scale as with the strings of an instrument, but in unison or in octaves, so that there might be no discords: for he was not devising any kind of plucking instrument, a lyre or zither, but one that was elementary, an Aeolian harp, to be performed on by the wind alone. The eye-sockets served as sound-holes bringing into play the resonance of the skull. To ensure that the harp turned to face every breath of wind, Friday attached two vulture's wings to it, causing Robinson to wonder how he had come by them, since the birds had always seemed to him invulnerable and immortal. He then hung the harp from the branch of a dead cypress standing starkly amid the waste of rock, in a place where every breeze must reach it. Indeed, no sooner was it hung than it emitted a thin, plaintive note, although the air seemed perfectly still. After listening for some minutes to this reedy lament Friday turned to Robinson with a grimace of scorn and two fingers raised to indicate that only two strings were sounding.

He had relapsed into his normal state of idleness, and Robinson had returned to his solar exercises, when eventually, after some weeks, Andoar gave of his best. One night Friday climbed the araucaria, where Robinson had made a nest for himself, using hides for screens, and tugged at his foot. A hot, thundery wind had risen which charged the air with electricity without bringing any promise of rain. The moon was sailing like a flung discus through thin wisps of cloud. Long before reaching the cypress Robinson heard strains of celestial music, as though an orchestra were playing, with flutes and violins. It was not a melody to pluck at the heart with its form and rhythm, but a single note, infinite in its harmonies, which took possession of the soul, a chord composed of countless elements in whose sustained power there was something fateful and implacable that held the hearer spellbound. The wind blew with increased strength as they drew near the singing tree. Tied on a short string to its topmost branch was the kite, throbbing like a drumskin, now suspended in trembling immobility, now furiously plunging. Andoar-the-flier hovered over Andoar-the-singer, seeming both to watch over him and to threaten him. Under the shifting light of the moon the vulture's wings attached to the mask flapped wildly, lending it a fantastic semblance of life in tune with the bluster of the storm. And over all sounded that powerful and melodious droning, music that was truly of the elements, inhuman music that was at once the deep voice of earth, the harmony of the spheres and the hoarse lament of the dead goat. Huddled together in the shelter of an overhanging boulder, Robinson and Friday lost all sense of themselves in the splendour of this mystery wherein the naked elements combined -- earth, tree and wind joined in celebrating the nocturnal apotheosis of Andoar.

Not long after this Robinson came upon the ditch where at one time he had condemned himself to penal labours for transgressing the island's laws. On these occasions he had also used it as an open air writing room, and he found, buried in the earth, a book of notes and observations belonging to his Journal, and two unused volumnes. The red ink in his small earthenware pot had long dried, and his vulture quill had disappeared. He had thought that everything was destroyed with the burning of the Residence. He told Friday of his discovery, resolved to continue writing the journal as a record of his progress. He thought about this for some days, and was on the point of collecting a new set of vulture's quills, and catching some more sea-porcupine for the ink, when Friday brought him a bundle of carefully-cut albatross quills and a pot of blue ink which he had made by crushing leaves of woad.

'Albatross now better than vulture,' he said simply, 'and blue better than red.'

Chapter 10

Pages from the Journal

This morning I rose before dawn, driven from my couch by a feeling of acute distress, and wandered through a world rendered desolate by the over-long absence of the sun, robbed of all colour and relief by the uniform grey light shed from a pallid sky. I climbed to the top of the rocks, wrestling with all the strength of my spirit against the weakness of my flesh. I must take care in future not to wake until the latest possible moment before sunrise. Sleep alone enables us to endure the long exile of the night, and no doubt this is the reason why it is bestowed on us.

Suspended above the sand-dunes to the east was a glow like that of a candlelit shrine wherein the rites attending the sun's epiphany were being mysteriously prepared. I knelt in contemplation with one knee on the ground, waiting while the nausea that had seized me was transformed into a mystical expectancy which I shared with the animals, the plants, the very stones. When I lifted my head it was as though the shrine had burst into flame, becoming a vast altar filling half the sky with its splendour of purple and gold. The first ray to start from it fell upon my red head like the protective hand of a father outstretched in benediction. The second ray purified my lips as once a burning coal had cleansed those of the prophet Isaiah. Two fiery swords then touched my shoulders and I rose to my feet, a knight of the sun. A shower of burning arrows pierced my face, breast and hands, and the grandiose ceremony of my consecration was completed by the thousand diadems and sceptres of light which bathed my more than human form.

Seated on a rock, Friday is patiently casting a line on to the ripple of the waters, fishing for gurnards. His bare feet, of which only the heels touch the rock, hang pointing downwards in an extension of the line of the legs. They are like long, narrow fins, very suited to his brown Triton-body. I reflect that whereas the South American Indians have small feet and thick calves, Friday has long feet and slender calves, a characteristic of his black race. Perhaps there is always an inverse proportion between those two parts of the body. The calf-muscles derive their purchase from the bone of the heel as from a lever. The longer the lever, the less the calf need work to flex the foot. This would explain the big calf and small foot of the yellow races, and the reverse in the case of the blacks.

O Sun, deliver me from the pull of gravity! Rid my blood of those dense humours which, though they protect me against extravagance and heedlessness, subdue the ardour of my youth and darken my joy in living. When I contemplate my sombre and melancholy northern face in the mirror I realize that the two meanings of the word *grace* – as applied to a dancer or to a saint – may become one under this Pacific sky. Instruct me in humour. Teach me lightness of heart, the smiling acceptance of the day's gifts, without calculation or gratitude or fear.

O Sun, cause me to resemble Friday. Give me Friday's smiling countenance, his face shaped for laughter. The high forehead sweeping back to be crowned with a garland of black curls. The eyes in which there is always a hint of derision, a touch of mockery defeated by the drollery of everything he sees. The curved, avid and animal mouth with its uptilted corners. The backward sway of his head on his shoulders, the better to laugh, to greet with laughter everything contained in the world; and the better to reject those two vices, obtuseness and malice.

But if my Aeolian comrade draws me to himself, O Sun, is it not that he may guide me towards you? Sun, are you pleased with me? Look at me. Is my transformation sufficiently in the manner of your own radiance? My beard, which pointed earthwards like a cluster of earthbound roots, has vanished, and now my head carries its glowing locks like a flame reaching upwards to the sky.

I am an arrow aimed at your heart, a sundial proclaiming with the shadow of my erect figure your mastery of the earth, as it measures your daily progress.

I am your upright witness upon earth, a sword tempered in your flame.

What has most changed in my life is the passing of time, its speed and even its direction. Formerly every day, hour and minute leaned in a sense towards the day, hour and minute that was to follow, and all were drawn into the pattern of the moment, whose transcience created a kind of vacuum. So time passed rapidly and usefully, the more quickly as it was usefully employed, leaving behind it an accumulation of achievement and wastage which was my history. Perhaps the sweep of time of which I was a part, after winding through millennia, would have 'coiled' and returned to its beginning. But the circularity of time remained the secret of the gods, and my own short life was no more than a segment, a straight line between two points aimed without meaning at infinity, like a path in a hedged garden that tells us nothing of the curve of the earth. Yet there are portents which offer us keys to eternity. There is the calendar, wherein the seasons eternally complete their cycle on a human scale, and even the modest circle of the hours.

For me the cycle has now shrunk until it is merged in the moment. The circular movement has become so swift that it cannot be distinguished from immobility. And it is as though, in consequence, my days had re-arranged themselves. No longer do they jostle on each other's heels. Each stands separate and upright, proudly affirming its own worth. And since they are no longer to be distinguished as the stages of a plan in process of execution, they so resemble each other as to be superimposed in my memory, so that I seem to be ceaselessly re-living the same day. Since the explosion destroyed my calendar-mast I have felt no need to record the passing of time. The memory of that accident and the events leading to it is imprinted on my mind with a vividness which in itself is evidence that time stopped when the water-clock was shattered. Are we not now living in eternity, Friday and I?

I have still not felt all the implications of this strange discovery. It must be noted at the outset that the revolution, sudden and literally explosive though it was, had been heralded and perhaps anticipated by certain happenings. For example, by my habit of stopping the water-clock when I wanted to escape from the tyrannous routine of the cultivated island. I did so at first to take refuge in its bowels as though escaping into timelessness. But was not the eternity which I looked for under the earth precisely what the explosion brought to its surface, which now sheds its benediction over all our boundaries? Or better, was not the explosion a volcanic release of the peace, imprisoned in the depths like a buried seed, which now prevails in the island, growing like a great tree to cast its shade over an area ever wider in extent? The more I reflect upon it, the more does it seem to me that the barrels of powder, Van Deyssel's pipe and Friday's misconduct were no more than an anecdote, a garment of happenings clothing a necessity that began to grow from the moment of the wreck of the *Virginia*.

There were also those moments of prophetic vision which with instinctive perception I termed my 'moments of innocence'. I seemed to glimpse *another island* hidden beneath the buildings and tilled fields which I had created on Speranza. Now I have been transported to that other Speranza, I am fixed in a moment of innocence. Speranza is no longer a virgin land which I must make fruitful, nor Friday a savage whom I must teach to behave. Both call for all my attention, a watchful and marvelling vigilance, for it seems to me – nay, I know it – that at every moment I am seeing them for the first time, and that nothing will ever dull their magical novelty.

I watch Friday as he walks towards me with his untroubled, steady pace over the shining sand of the lagoon, and the emptiness of sea and sky is so vast that I have no scale by which to measure him, so that he might be a figure three inches high within reach of my hand or a ten-foot giant half a mile away.

Here he comes. Shall I ever learn to walk with his natural majesty? Do I sound absurd if I say that he seems clothed by his nakedness? He carries his body like a sovereign affirmation, he bears himself like a monstrance of flesh. His animal beauty proclaims itself, seeming to create a nothingness around it.

He leaves the lagoon and comes towards me as I sit on the beach. But from the moment when he treads the dry sand with its litter of broken shells, and as he passes between a rock and a tuft of purple seaweed, becoming again a part of our familiar landscape, his beauty wears another aspect. It becomes grace. He smiles at me and, raising his hand in a gesture like that of an angel in a religious painting, points to the sky, where the south-westerly breeze is dispelling the clouds that have accumulated during the past several days, to restore the untrammelled reign of the sun. He gives a skip, bringing into play the ripple of his muscles. He comes up to me but says nothing, a silent companion. He turns to look over the lagoon he has just crossed, while his spirit seems to hover amid the mists that mark the end of an unsettled day, leaving his body planted on the sand with its legs apart. Seated near him I note the part of his leg situated behind the knee, its pearly lightness and the pattern it forms, a capital H. It is like a throat, firm and smooth when the leg is stretched, soft and hollow when it bends.

I put my hands on his knees, making of them cups to fit the shape of the knee and feel its life. In its hardness and dryness, by contrast with the softness of the thigh, the knee is the key of the vault on which the earthly frame is borne, raising it aloft in a living equilibrium to the sky. There is no movement of the body, no tremor, no impulse of hesitation, that does not proceed from that warm, moving disc and return to it. During several seconds my hands learn that Friday's motionless stance is not that of a stone or tree-stump, but the quivering outcome, constantly varied and readjusted, of a series of actions and reactions, the play of all his muscles.

Walking in the dusk at the edge of the marshland I see a small animal coming towards me, reminding me at first of our poor Tenn. Then I see that it is a plump female agouti. I am downwind from it, and the little creature, which is naturally short-sighted, continues to approach without suspecting my presence. I try to turn myself into a rock or tree-stump, hoping it will pass me by and go on its way. But no. Within a few yards of me it becomes suddenly rigid, ears cocked and head turned towards me with big, cloudy eyes. And then it is off like lightning, darting madly, not into the reeds, where it could vanish in an instant, but back along the path by which it came. I can still hear the scrabble of its claws on the stones when it has become no more than a bounding shadow.

I try to imagine that animal's world, dominated by the sense of smell as sight dominates the world of men. The strength and direction of the wind, so little important to us, are a fundamental part of it. The creature exists in the overlap between two unequally distinguishable zones – unequally 'lighted', in human terms. The one is the darker because the other – the zone of the wind – teems with odours. In the absence of wind the two halves of the world merge in a confused twilight, but at the least breeze the zone of wind glows with a light that turns to inky blackness when the breeze has passed. An immensely sensitive power of discrimation, comparable to the lens of the human eye, enables the scents in the windy zone to be distinguished at a great distance, whether it be the scent of a particular tree, of a peccary or a parrot, or of Friday on the way back to his pepper-trees chewing an araucaria nut – and with the richness that is proper to the sense of smell. I think of Tenn when Friday was digging those holes in the ground, how he thrust his nose into the depths of the fresh-turned soil, truly intoxicated at that moment, running and leaping in circles round the digger and yelping with excitement and delight – so absorbed in his pursuit of smells that for him there was nothing else.

As I think of it, there is nothing very astonishing in the almost crazed intensity with which I watch Friday. What is unbelievable is that I should have lived so long with him without, so to speak, seeing him at all. How account for that blind indifference, when for me he is the whole of humanity assembled in one person, my son and my father, my brother and my neighbour, my nearest and my farthest? I must concentrate every emotion that man feels for his fellows upon this sole 'other', because what would otherwise become of my ability to feel? What should I do with pity and hatred, admiration and fear, if Friday did not inspire those emotions in me? That the fascination he holds for me is largely reciprocated is something of which I have received many proofs. Two days ago he came up to me while I lay drowsing on the beach. He stood for some moments gazing at me, a dark, slender figure outlined against the brilliant sky. Then he knelt down beside me and began to examine me with an extraordinary intentness. His fingers wandered over my face, patted my cheeks, followed the curve of my chin, tested the flexibility of my nose. He made me raise my arms above my head, and bending over my body he explored it inch by inch like an anatomist preparing to dissect a corpse. He seemed to have forgotten that I lived and breathed, that thoughts might enter my head, that I might grow impatient. But, understanding all too well the thirst for humankind by which he was moved, I made no attempt to stop him. In the end he smiled as though awaking from a dream and was suddenly conscious of my presence; he laid his finger on a blue vein visible beneath my tanned skin and said in a tone of mock-apology, 'Oh! I can see your blood!'

Am I returning to the sun-cult which was a part of paganism? I think not. I know little of the beliefs and observances of those legendary 'pagans', who perhaps never existed except in the imagination of our religious instructors. But it is true that, in a state of intolerable solitude that threatened to drive me to madness or suicide, I instinctively looked elsewhere for the support which the company of men no longer afforded me. The disciplines and modes of thought I had derived from commerce with my fellows crumbled and vanished. I groped about me, seeking salvation in communion with the elements, having myself become elemental. The earth of Speranza brought a first solution which seemed workable and lasting, although it was not without imperfections and dangers. Then Friday came, and while seeming to acquiesce in my earthly order, did everything in his power to undermine it. But there was another way. Although the earth repelled him, Friday was as much elemental by nature as I had become by force of circumstance. Under his influence, and the successive blows he dealt me, I have travelled the road of a long and painful metamorphosis. The man of earth dragged from his labours by a spirit of the air could not of himself become a creature of air. He was too dense in substance, too sluggish in his movements. But the sun with its wand of light touched the soft, white grub sunk in the shadow of the earth, and the grub has grown into a moth with a corselet of metal, its wings dusted with gold, a creature of the sun, hard and impervious to the elements, but of a terrifying weakness when the rays of the sun-god are not there to sustain it.

*

Andoar was myself. I myself was that solitary and stubborn old male, with his patriarch's beard and his fleece sweating lubricity, that faun of earth harshly rooted through his four cloven hooves to the rock hillside. Friday conceived a strange friendship for him, and a cruel game ensued between them. 'I will make Andoar fly and sing,' Friday mysteriously declared. But to turn the old goat into a spirit of air, what ordeals did he inflict on his remains!

The Aeolian harp. Wholly absorbed in the present, and abhorring any task that must proceed by long, patient stages, Friday, with an infallible instinct, chose the one instrument corresponding to his own nature. The Aeolian harp is not merely an elemental instrument drawing song from the winds: it is also the only instrument whose music does not need time for its development but exists entirely in the movement. You may increase the number of its strings and tune them to whatever notes you will, but still you are composing an *instant symphony* whose first and last chord sounds whenever the wind touches the harp.

I watch Friday as he dives amid the breakers rolling up on to the beach; and the kind of dance in which he is engaged, the natural grace and elegance of his movements, the gaiety, the gleam of wet, firm flesh, all this brings to my mind the thought of Venus rising from the waves.

This is one of the many threads of significance centred upon Friday which I seek to disentangle, and it is related even to the name I have bestowed on him. Friday, if I am not mistaken, is in its ancient meaning the day of Venus. To Christians it is the day of the death of Christ. I cannot help feeling that in this conjunction, fortuitous though it may be, there is a mystery beyond my grasp, and one which shocks what is left of the devout Puritan I once was.

Another thread is contained in the last words spoken to me before the wreck of the *Virginia*. Since they were in some sort a spiritual viaticum bestowed on me by mankind before it abandoned me to the elements, they should be imprinted on my memory in letters of fire; but the truth, alas, is that I can recall nothing of them but a few fragments. I mean, of course, the predictions which Captain Pieter Van Deyssel read, or professed to read, in the tarot-cards. The name of Venus occurred several times in that utterance which so disconcerted the young man I then was. I seem to remember the Captain saying that I should become a hermit in a cave, to be lured out of it by the coming of Venus; but then, I fancy, this visitant from the sea changed into an archer shooting arrows at the sun. This, however, was not the most important part. I have a confused recollection of a card depicting two children – twins and innocents – standing hand in hand outside a wall symbolizing the City of the Sun. At this point Van Deyssel talked about circular sexuality closing upon itself, and he likened it to a serpent biting its own tail.

As to my sexuality, I may note that at no time has Friday inspired me with any sodomite desire. For one thing, he came too late, when my sexuality had already become elemental and was directed towards Speranza. But above all, Venus, or Aphrodite, did not emerge from the waves and tread my shores in order to seduce me, but to drive me into the realm of her father, Uranus, the 'sky crowned with stars', whose bleeding genitals, severed from his body and cast into the sea, broke into a white foam from which the goddess was born. It was not a matter of turning me back to human loves but, while leaving me still an elemental, causing me to change my element. This has now happened. My love-affair with Speranza was still largely human in its nature; I fecundated her soil as though I were lying with a wife. It was Friday who brought about the deeper change. The harsh stab of desire that pierces the loins of the lover has been transformed for me into soft jubilation which exalts and pervades me from head to foot, so long as the sun-god bathes me in his rays. There is no longer that loss of substance which leaves the animal, *post coitum*, sad. My sky-love floods me with a vital energy which endows me with strength for a day and a night. If this is to be translated into human language, I must consider myself feminine and the bride of the sky. But that kind of anthropomorphism is meaningless. The truth is that at the height to which Friday and I have soared difference of sex is left behind. Friday may be identified with Venus, just as I may be said, in human terms, to open my body to the embrace of the sun.

The full moon is so bright that I can write these lines without the aid of a lamp. Friday is asleep, curled up in a ball at my feet.

The atmosphere of unreality, with familiar objects lost in shadow – the starkness – lends a levity and inconsequence to my thoughts which they atone for by the speed of their passing. This meditation will be no more than a sighing of the moon. *Ave spiritu*, the thoughts that are about to die salute you!

The Goddess of Fantasy hangs like a milky bubble in a sky which her own rays have swept clean of stars. Her round shape is flawless, but it is as though her substance were in turmoil, spinning in a manner to suggest that some hidden process of creation is at work within her. Vague outlines appear and vanish on the white disc, shadowy hands reach and clasp, faces smile for an instant, to vanish into mist. The spinning gains in speed until it resembles immobility, as though the very excess of that turbulence had caused the lunar jelly to set. And gradually the pattern is defined. There are poles at either end of the egg, with a tracery of lines between them. The poles become heads and the arabesque the outline of two conjoined bodies. Two similar beings, twins, are in process of gestation; Gemini are being born on the moon. Linked together they gently move, as though awakening after a centuries long sleep. Their movements, which at first are like soft and drowsy caresses, suddenly change, and now they are struggling to detach themselves from one another. Each strives with his dense, obsessive shadow like a child fighting to escape from the cloying darkness of the womb. At length they separate and, ravished and solitary, reach out to rediscover their fraternal intimacy. In Leda's egg, fecundated by Jupiter, the Swan, the Dioscuri are born, Castor and Pollux, the Twins of the Sun, more intimately linked than human twins because they share a single soul. Human twins are two-souled, Gemini are one-souled. In consequence they are endowed with an unequalled density of flesh, half as much inhabited by spirit, half as porous, twice as heavy and fleshy as that of human twins. This it is that gives them their eternal youth and their in-human beauty, which is the beauty of glass and metal and shining surfaces, a glitter that is not living. They are not links in a chain running from generation to generation through the vicissitudes of history. They are the Dioscuri, beings fallen like meteors from heaven. The Sun, their father, blesses them, his flame envelopes them and bestows on them the gift of eternity . . .

A small cloud coming from the west has covered Leda's egg. Friday looks up at me with a dreaming face, mutters a few disjointed, rapid words, and then sinks back into slumber, legs drawn defensively up to his belly and fists clenched on either side of his dark head. Venus, the Swan, Leda, the Twins . . . I grope in search of myself in this forest of allegory.

Chapter 11

Friday was gathering blossoms of myrtle with which to make an infusion when he saw a white speck on the eastern horizon. He ran at once to tell Robinson, who was shaving. If Robinson was agitated by the news he did not show it.

'So we are going to have visitors,' he said simply. 'All the more reason why I should complete my toilet.'

In a state of high excitement Friday climbed to the top of the rocks, taking with him the spyglass. The ship was a topsail schooner under a full head of sail, making at a speed of perhaps a dozen knots in the stiff, south-westerly breeze, for the marshy side of the island. Friday ran back to report this to Robinson, who was now putting the finishing touches to his sun-bleached locks with a tortoiseshell comb, and then returned to his observation post. The vessel had gone over on to the starboard tack, evidently because her captain realized that this side of the island was not suitable for landing, and under shortened sail was proceeding on a course parallel with the coast. Friday hurried to tell Robinson that she was passing the sand-dunes and would presumably fetch up in the Bay of Salvation. The first thing was to ascertain her nationality. Together they ran to the edge of the trees bordering the beach, and Robinson studied her through the spyglass. She was now turning into the wind two cables' lengths offshore; her sails were coming down and they heard the rattle of the anchor-chain.

She was a vessel of a kind unfamiliar to Robinson, evidently of recent design, but she was flying the colours of his Britannic Majesty. Accordingly Robinson emerged from his concealment and walked on to the beach with the composure proper to a monarch welcoming visitors to his realm. He watched while a longboat was lowered in a splash of spray and a party of men headed for the shore.

As he stood gazing at the sweep of the oars Robinson was suddenly conscious of the enormous weight of the few moments that remained before the man in the bows staved off the first rocks with his boathook. He had a vision, like that of a drowning man, of his whole life on the island – the building of the *Escape*, the mire, the frenetic cultivation of Speranza, the cave, the combe, the coming of Friday, the explosion – above all, the measureless extent of time during which his conversion to the sun had been completed in tranquil happiness.

There were a number of casks in the boat, which was evidently coming ashore for water, and standing in the stern-sheets, top-booted and armed, was a black-bearded man wearing a straw hat. He was the forerunner of the community of mankind which was now to enmesh Robinson in the tangle of its words and deeds, and restore him to the great complex of civilization. The world so patiently woven and elaborated during the long years of solitude would be tested to the uttermost when Robinson's hand clasped that of this envoy of humanity.

There was a grating sound as the boat grounded, and the sailors jumped out and pulled her up on to the beach, out of reach of the rising tide. The bearded man held out his hand to Robinson.

'William Hunter, captain of the schooner *Heron*, from Liverpool.'

'What is the date?' asked Robinson.

The Captain turned in surprise to the man standing beside him, who seemed to be the mate.

'What's the date, Joe?'

'December 19th, sir.'

'But the year?' demanded Robinson. 'The year?'

'Why, it's 1787.'

Robinson made a rapid calculation. The *Virginia* had been wrecked on 30 September 1759 – that was to say, twenty-eight years, two months and an unspecified number of days ago. Despite all the things that had happened, and the extent of the change in himself, he found this vast span of time almost unbelievable. He could not venture to ask if they were sure of the year, which to him was like a date in the still distant future. Indeed he resolved instantly not to tell them the date of the wreck of the *Virginia*, from a kind of apprehension, a fear that they would not believe him or would treat him as a phenomenon.

'I was cast ashore on this island by the wreck of the brig *Virginia*, commanded by Captain Pieter Van Deyssel of Flushing,' he said. 'I was the only survivor. The shock has played tricks with my memory, and I cannot remember what year it was.'

'I don't recall the loss of a vessel of that name,' said Hunter. 'But the war with America has greatly affected maritime relations.'

Robinson knew nothing of this war. He saw that he would need to exercise great prudence if he was to conceal his ignorance of what had been happening in the world.

Friday meanwhile, after helping the boat's crew to unload their casks, was guiding them to the nearest stream. Robinson was struck by the ease with which he had got on terms with this party of foreigners, while he himself felt so remote from their captain. Evidently Friday was ingratiating himself with them because he hoped to be taken on board the *Heron*; nor could Robinson deny that he, too, was eager to visit the fine fore-and-aft rigged vessel with her low, raking lines, so clearly built for speed. But at the same time these men and the world they brought with them caused him an overwhelming discomfort which he was struggling to over-come. He was still alive. He had triumphed over madness during his years of solitude. He had achieved a state of stability, or series of states, in which he and Speranza, and then Speranza, Friday and himself had formed a unity which endured and had brought supreme happiness. After much suffering and many fateful crises he now felt able, with Friday at his side, to defy the passage of time and, like a meteor launched fictionless in space, to continue indefinitely on his course without weariness or loss of momentum. Never-theless, a confrontation with other men was a supreme test that might enable him to accomplish even more. It might be that, returning to England, he would contrive not only to preserve the solar happiness he had attained but to make of it a source of higher power in the city of men. Thus had Zoroaster, after forging his soul in the heat of the desert sun, returned to dispense his wisdom to the corrupt turmoil of mankind.

Meanwhile he was laboriously engaged with Hunter in a conversation which threatened to dissolve in uneasy silence. He had volunteered to show him what the island had to offer in the way of game, fresh fruits and vegetables as a protection against scurvy, and two of the sailors were already climbing coconut palms to cut down nuts while others could be heard shouting as they hunted the goats. Robinson re-flected, not without pride, on the acute distress it would have caused him in the days of the cultivated island to see it pil-laged in this fashion. It was not so much the senseless muti-lation of the trees or the heedless slaughter of the animals that now troubled him, but the coarse and avaricious bearing of these men who were his fellows, so familiar to him and yet so strange. The place where Speranza's counting-house had once stood was now overgrown with tall grass that swayed with a silken rustle in the wind; and here one of the sailors had discovered two pieces of gold. He shouted to his comrades and after an excited dispute they resolved to set fire to the grass in the hope of finding more. The fact that the gold in a sense belonged to him scarcely occurred to Robinson, nor did he give much thought to the animals who were to be deprived of the only pasture which the rainy season did not turn into a swamp. He was too absorbed in listening to the quarrels that broke out with each new discovery, and he paid little attention to the Captain, who was telling him how during the war he had sunk a French troopship carrying reinforcements to the American rebels. The mate, on Robinson's other side, was talking about the slave-trade and the huge profits to be derived from it. Both men were absorbed in their own preoccupations, and neither thought of questioning him about his life on the island. Even the presence of Friday did not seem to interest them. And Robinson knew that in former times he had been as they were, driven by the same motives of greed, arrogance and violence, and that a part of him was still at one with them. Thinking this, he continued to observe them with the detachment of a naturalist studying a colony of bees or ants, or the dubious forms of life that are to be found under a stone.

Each of these men was a *possible* world, having its own coherence, its values, its sources of attraction and repulsion, its centre of gravity. And with all the differences between them, each of these possible worlds at that moment shared a vision, casual and superficial, of the island of Speranza, which caused them to act in common, and which incidentally contained a shipwrecked man called Robinson and his half-caste servant. For the present this picture occupied their minds, but for each of them it was purely temporary, destined very soon to be returned to the limbo from which it had been briefly plucked by the accident of the *Heron*'s getting off course. And each of these possible worlds naïvely proclaimed itself the reality. That was what other people were: the possible obstinately passing for the real. All Robinson's upbringing had taught him that to reject the affirmation was cruel, egotistical and immoral; but this was an attitude of mind that he had lost during the years, and now he wondered if he could ever recover it. Mingled with the claims of those possible worlds to exist was their picture of a Speranza doomed to disappear, and it seemed to him that in allowing them the dignity they strove to assert he was vowing Speranza to destruction.

The boat had gone off to the schooner, loaded to the gunwales with fruit, game, vegetables and a few living but hamstrung goats. It now returned, and the crew stood by awaiting orders.

'You will of course do me the honour of dining with me,' the Captain said; and without waiting for Robinson's reply he instructed the men to take the fresh water to the ship and then come back to fetch them. Being left alone with Robinson he shed something of the reserve he had maintained since landing and talked, not without bitterness, of his life during the past four years.

As a youthful and enthusiastic naval officer he had fought under Admiral Howe in the war of American Independence and had distinguished himself at the battle of Brooklyn and the capture of New York; but he had been quite unprepared for the reverses that had followed those early successes.

'Young Service officers are taught to think in terms of nothing but victory,' he said. 'It would be wiser to teach them to recover from defeat. To be routed and regroup one's forces, or to be forced to break off a sea-action with spars and rigging shot to pieces, and carry out repairs at sea and turn back to re-engage the enemy – nothing can be harder than that. But it is an art that our leaders think it shameful to teach us, although we learn from the history books that many great victories have sprung from defeat, and every stableboy knows that the horse that leads at the start of the race is most likely to be beaten at the post.'

The British defeat at Saratoga, which had brought France into the war on the side of the colonists, and France's sea victories off Grenada and Tobago, had inspired Hunter with a lively hatred of the French; and the shame of the eventual British capitulation, the surrender of what was then the brightest jewel in the English crown, had caused him to resign his commission.

For a time he had sailed as a master of merchantmen, but the prosaic squalor of the trader's life, the greed of ship-owners, the bills of lading, the stowage and unloading of cargoes that were often suspect, the chaffering with customs and excise men – none of this had suited him. When he was on the verge of giving up the sea altogether a stroke of luck had befallen him – the only one, he added, in his life. He had been offered the command of the *Heron*, whose light build and speedy lines rendered her peculiarly suitable for the carrying of less bulky cargoes – tea, spices, rare metals, precious stones and opium   a trade entailing long voyages, with a spice of mystery and adventure that appealed to his romantic nature. Perhaps he might have been happier still as a buccaneer or freebooter, but his naval training had left him with an instinctive aversion from activities of the more disreputable kind.

When Robinson jumped down on to the deck of the *Heron* he was greeted by a radiant Friday who had been brought on board on the boat's previous trip. He had evidently been made a pet of by the ship's company and he seemed as much at home as if he had spent his life on her. Robinson had had occasion to note in the past that the only human devices which impressed primitive peoples were things coming within their scope, such as knives, clothes, small boats. Beyond this they were unmoved, as though a mansion or rigged ship were a work of nature, no more to be marvelled at than a cavern or an iceberg. It was not so with Friday, and Robin-

son at first assumed that the Araucanian's ready understanding of everything he saw was due to his own influence. But
as he watched him run like a monkey up the shrouds and
stand laughing on the cross-trees, fifty feet above deck, he
thought of Friday's airy contrivances – the arrows, the kite
and the harp – and realized that for him this sailing-ship
which was so graceful and handsomely rigged represented a
supreme conquest of the air. The thought saddened him,
the more so since he was conscious of a growing revulsion in
himself from this world into which he was being dragged,
as he felt, against his will.

His unhappiness was increased by the sight of a small,
half-naked figure crouched at the foot of one of the masts, to
which it was tied. It was a boy of about twelve, lean as a
skinned cat. His face was hidden. A thick mass of red hair
made his narrow shoulders with their sharp shoulder-blades
seem even more brittle, and there was a series of broad
weals, some bleeding slightly, across his back.

'That's Jan, the galley-boy,' Hunter said. He turned and
asked: 'What's he been doing now?'

In answer to the question a round, red face, that of the
ship's cook, shot up through the galley-hatch like a jack-in-
the-box.

'He spoilt the pastry I was making by salting it three times
over,' the cook growled. 'He never thinks what he's doing.
I've given him a touch of the rope's-end and he'll get more if
he doesn't mend his ways.'

'Better untie him,' the Captain said. 'We shall want him
to wait at table.'

Robinson dined in the Captain's cabin with Hunter and
the first mate. He did not see what became of Friday, who
was presumably eating with the crew. Sustaining the conversation was not difficult. His hosts seemed to have made up
their minds that he had everything to learn and nothing of
consequence to tell them about Friday or himself, and the

convenient assumption enabled him to observe and reflect at leisure. It was of course true, in a sense, that he had everything to learn, or rather to assimilate and digest; but what he heard was to him as heavy and indigestible as the food on his plate, and he feared lest a sudden attack of nausea should cause him to vomit not only this but the whole world he was encountering.

What principally repelled him was not so much the coarse brutality, the greeds and animosities that emerged with a naïve unawareness from the discourse of these two civilized and perfectly honourable men. It was easy to believe that they could have been men of a different stamp, mild-mannered, benevolent and generous. For Robinson the evil went deeper, and he defined it to himself as the incurable pettiness, in relation to life, of the ends which all men so feverishly pursued. Each was in search of something, some especial acquisition, wealth or personal satisfaction; but why that thing more than another? None could have told him. He imagined himself asking Hunter, for example, 'What do you live for?' Hunter would have had no reply, and no recourse but to ask the question in return; and Robinson would have answered it by pointing with one hand to the shores of Speranza and with the other to the sun. After a moment of stupefaction Hunter would have burst out laughing, the laughter of folly in the face of wisdom: for what was the sun to him but a gigantic flame? How could he conceive of it as possessing a spirit that could radiate with eternity those who had learnt to open their hearts to it?

The boy, Jan, was waiting on them, half-hidden behind a large, white apron. His small, bony, freckled face looked smaller still under the tangled mop of hair, and Robinson tried to meet his eyes, which were so blue that it was as though the sky were shining through his head. But he paid scant attention to the visitor, being too terrified of making some blunder as he served them. Hunter had the habit, after speaking a few words with a sort of controlled vehemence, of lapsing into a moody or disdainful silence, like the garrison of a besieged fortress, which after damaging the enemy with a sudden sortie returns hastily to the shelter of its walls. The gaps were filled by the discourse of the mate, Joseph, who, entirely concerned with practical matters and the newest developments in the art of navigation, evidently felt for his commander a warm esteem sustained by a total lack of comprehension. It was he, when the meal was over, who took Robinson on deck, leaving the Captain below. He was particularly anxious to show him the ship's sextant, the novel appliance whereby the altitude of the sun could be observed, and latitude and longitude determined, with an accuracy incomparably greater than that of the old quadrant method. Robinson was interested by the enthusiastic lecture and it gave him pleasure to handle the gleaming brass and ivory instrument, but what principally struck him was the display of liveliness in a mind that was otherwise so circumscribed. Intelligence and stupidity could live together in the same head, mixing no more than oil and water. When he was talking of index- and horizon-glasses, of the vernier scale and angles of incidence, Joseph glowed with intelligence; but only a few minutes before he had been saying of the boy, Jan, that he had no call to complain of a whipping, because his mother was nothing but a dockside whore.

The sun was beginning to decline. It was the hour when Robinson was accustomed to bathe in its rays in order to store himself with energy and warmth before the shadows lengthened and the evening breeze caused the eucalyptus trees along the beach to whisper among themselves. At Joseph's suggestion he stretched himself on the poop-deck and lay for a long time watching the trunk of the topmast as it described invisible patterns in a deep blue sky where a slender crescent moon hung like a shred of transparent porcelain. He turned his head to look at Speranza, the pale line of sand at the water's edge and the rising flow of greenery leading to the jagged rock beyond. Then it was that he bowed to the decision that all day had been forming within him, the inexorable resolve to let the *Heron* sail without him and to remain on the island with Friday. It was a compulsion due, even more than to the gulf that separated him from the men aboard that ship, to his panic rejection of the degrading and mortal turbulence of the times in which they lived, and which they spread around them. 19 December 1787. Twenty-eight years, two months and some twenty days. The figure still amazed him. Had he not been cast ashore on Speranza he would now be in his fifties, a greybeard with creaking bones. His children would be older than he had been when he left them, and perhaps he would be a grandfather. But none of these things had happened to him. Speranza lay only two cables distant from the ship and the miasma that pervaded it, a glowing denial of that sinister degradation. The truth was that he was younger today than the pious and self-seeking young man who had set sail in the *Virginia*, not young with a biological youth, corruptible and harbouring the seeds of its decrepitude, but with a mineral youth, solar and divine. Every day was for him a first beginning, an absolute beginning of the history of the world. Beneath the rays of the sun-god, Speranza trembled in an eternal present, without past or future. He could not forsake that everlasting instant poised at the needle-point of a perfect ecstasy, to sink back into a world of usury, dust and decay.

When he announced his intention of staying on the island only Joseph seemed surprised. Hunter merely smiled coldly. Perhaps he was relieved at not having to burden himself with two passengers in a ship where there was little room to spare. He had the courtesy to treat the supplies he had brought on board as though they had been the property of Robinson, the master of the island, and he offered him in exchange a gig

13

which he carried lashed on the poop-deck and which was additional to the ship's normal complement of boats. It was a handy little craft, more seaworthy than Robinson's aged canoe, and he and Friday rowed themselves ashore in it as darkness fell.

Robinson's joy at repossessing the realm which he had thought lost to him for ever was reflected in the last red glow of the sunset. Immense though his comfort was, there was a hint of funeral solemnity in the peace that surrounded him. He felt, not hurt but aged, as though his visit to the *Heron* had marked the end of a very long and happy youth. Yet what did this matter? The English ship would weigh anchor by the first light of dawn, and resume her wandering course guided by the whim of her shadowy commander. The waters of the Bay of Salvation would close over the wake of the only vessel that had entered them in twenty-eight years. Robinson had let it be known that he would prefer the whereabouts of the island not to be revealed, and the wish was too much in accordance with Hunter's own strange character for him not to respect it. Thus the matter was closed, the daylong interlude that had brought tumult and upheaval to the Twins' eternity.

Chapter 12

Dawn was still pallid in the sky when Robinson climbed down from his nest in the araucaria. He had formed the habit of sleeping until the last minutes before sunrise, to reduce as far as possible that mournful period of waiting, the most lifeless in the twenty-four hours because the furthest removed from sunset. But the unaccustomed food, the wine, and the deep-seated unease in himself, had rendered his slumber feverish, with sudden starts and periods of unfruitful wakefulness. Lying in darkness, he had been the defenceless prey of old thoughts and tormenting obsessions. He rose early to escape the turmoil in his mind.

He walked on to the beach. As he had expected, the *Heron* was gone. The sea was grey under a colourless sky, and the weight of a heavy dew caused plants to bow their heads in a pale luminosity that was neither light nor shade but mercilessly clear. Even the birds were silent. Robinson felt a hollow of despair growing in him, a black, resounding emptiness like a spirit of evil that filled his heart with sickness and his mouth with a bitter juice. A wave ran sluggishly up the beach, toyed for an instant with the body of a dead crab, and then withdrew as though in disappointment. In a little while, an hour at the most, the sun would shine, restoring life and joy to all things, and to Robinson. He must hold out until then, and resist the temptation to awaken Friday.

There could be no doubt that the coming of the *Heron* had gravely disturbed the delicate balance of the trio they formed, Robinson, Friday and Speranza. Speranza's wounds were but superficial and would vanish in a few months; but how long would it take Friday to forget the swift, graceful ship so tender to every touch of the wind? Robinson now reproached himself for having decided to remain on the island without first speaking of the matter to Friday. Well, today he would tell him what he had learned from Joseph of the horrors of the slave-trade and the life that awaited the blacks in the plantations of the New World. Friday's regrets, if he had any, would thereby be lessened.

Thinking of this he moved automatically in the direction of the two pepper-trees between which Friday's hammock was slung. He did not mean to wake him but only to watch him as he slept, to draw comfort from the innocent tranquility of his presence.

The hammock was empty. What was more surprising was the absence of the trifles with which Friday was accustomed to amuse himself – a piece of mirror, his blowpipe, a reed-pipe, a handful of feathers and so on. Robinson ran down to the beach again. The gig and the canoe were both there, drawn up on the foreshore. But surely if Friday had gone back to the *Heron*, he would have taken one of them.

Robinson began to search the island, calling Friday's name. Running, stumbling and shouting, he hastened from the Bay of Salvation to the eastern sand-dunes, from the cave to the pink combe, from the woodlands on the western side to the lagoon, with the growing, despairing conviction that this was all in vain. He did not understand Friday's desertion, but he could not escape the evidence that he was alone on the island, as alone as he had been at the beginning. The frantic search completed his demoralization by taking him to places he had not visited for months. He felt the crumbling remains of the *Escape* under his hands and the tepid warmth of the mire beneath his feet. He found near the place of the Residence a part of the charred leather binding of his Bible. All the pages had been burnt, excepting

a fragment containing the first lines of the *Book of Kings;*
and in a mist of weakness he read:

Now King David was old and stricken in years; and they
covered him with clothes, but he gat no heat.

Wherefore his servants said unto him, Let there be sought
for my lord the king a young virgin: and let her stand before
the king, and let her cherish him, and let her lie in thy bosom,
that my lord the king may get heat.

Robinson perceived that the twenty-eight years which
until yesterday had not existed had now closed down upon
him. The *Heron* had brought them with her like the germs
of a mortal disease and he was suddenly an old man. He
realized also that for an old man there is no greater affliction
than solitude. '*Let her lie in thy bosom, that my lord the*
king may get heat.' Indeed he was shivering with cold in
the dew of the morning, and never again would there be
anyone to warm him. He came upon a last relic, Tenn's
collar, mouldy with damp. All the years which had seemed
to be abolished were recalled by their prosaic and heart-
rendering vestiges. He pressed his forehead against the trunk
of a cypress and his lips quivered, but old men do not weep.
His stomach heaved and he vomited the winey remains of
the meal he had eaten on board the ship. When he looked
up he found himself surrounded by a circle of vultures,
standing only a few yards distant and gazing at him with
pink eyes. They too had to keep this appointment with the
past.

Was he now to begin all over again – the tilled fields, the
breeding-pens, the buildings – while he awaited the coming
of another Friday who would sweep it all away in a burst of
flame and raise him again to the heights? A mockery! The
truth was that now his only choice was between time and
eternity. Eternal rebirth, that bastard offspring of both, was
but a form of madness. There was only one way of salvation:
he must seek to regain that timeless limbo, peopled by in-

nocents, which he had gradually attained and from which the visit of the *Heron* had caused him to fall. But how, being old and without strength, could he hope to recover that state of grace that was so slow and difficult of achievement? How could it happen, except simply by the act of dying? Was not this the only eternity that remained to him, death on this island where perhaps for decades no other person would ever come? But he must outwit the vultures, who seemed to be mysteriously aware of what was taking place and waited to perform their funeral office. His bones must whiten beneath the stones of Speranza like spillikins whose assemblage no one must disturb. That would be a fitting end to the strange and unsung tale of the solitary of Speranza.

He made his way slowly to the mound of rock which had buried the mouth of the cave, feeling sure that by wriggling between the boulders he could bury himself deeply enough to escape any animal visitation. Perhaps by the exercise of extreme patience he might even penetrate into the cave itself and down to that lowest recess. There he need only huddle like a foetus and close his eyes for life to slip away from him, so utter was his weariness, so deep his despair.

He found a crevice scarcely larger than a rabbit's burrow but which, in his diminished state, he felt he could crawl through. He was examining it to see how far it went when he thought he heard a sound of movement. A pebble rattled in the depths, and the mouth of the crevice was obstructed by a body. After some wriggling it emerged, and a child stood before Robinson with one arm shielding his face – against the daylight or against a blow. Robinson stepped back, dumbfounded.

'Who are you?' he asked. 'What are you doing here?'

'I was the cook's boy aboard the *Heron*,' the child replied. 'I was unhappy. I saw you look at me when I was waiting at table, and your eyes were kind. When I heard that you were not going to sail with us I determined to escape to this island to be with you. Last night, when I was about to lower myself over the side and swim ashore, I saw a man come aboard from a canoe. It was your native servant. He cast the canoe adrift and went straight to the mate's cabin, where the mate seemed to be expecting him. So then I guessed that he intended to stay on board. I swam to the canoe and paddled to the island. I have been hiding here ever since. And,' the child concluded on a note of triumph, 'the *Heron* has sailed without me.'

'Come with me,' said Robinson.

He took the boy by the hand and together they began to climb the slope leading to the sharp peak of rock which was the highest point of the island. Halfway up Robinson stopped and turned to look at the boy. The light blue eyes with pale albino lashes gazed up at him, and the boy smiled faintly. Robinson opened his hand to examine the hand it was clasping, and was touched to see it so slender and frail-seeming, yet calloused by the rough work of the ship.

'I'm going to show you something,' he said in the effort to control his emotions, without quite knowing what he intended.

The island at their feet was partly shrouded in mist, but a glow had begun to appear amid the grey of the eastern sky. The gig and the canoe were beginning to stir slightly as the rising tide lapped round them. To the north a gleam of white was speeding towards the horizon, and Robinson pointed towards it.

'Look well at it,' he said. 'A ship within sight of Speranza. It is something you may never see again.'

The gleam grew smaller and was presently lost in the distance, and it was at this moment that the sun loosed its first arrows. A cricket chirped. A gull swooped down to the mirror-surface of the sea, and a moment later soared upwards with broad wings flapping and a silver fish in its beak. The sky in an instant had become pale blue. The flowers which had hung with their closed petals bowing to the west now turned and spread them wide towards the east, and the song of birds and insects rose in the air. Robinson had forgotten the boy. Drawn up to his full height he was confronting the solar ecstasy with a joy that was almost painful, while the bright splendour in which he bathed washed him clean of the grime of the past day and night. A blade of fire seemed to penetrate his flesh, causing his whole being to tremble. Speranza was shedding her veil of mist, to emerge unsullied and intact. Indeed, it was as though the agony and the nightmare had never taken place. Eternity, reasserting its hold on him, had effaced that ugly but trivial interlude. He drew a deep breath, filled with the sense of utter contentment, and his chest swelled like a breastplate of brass. His feet were solidly planted on the rock, and his legs sturdy and unshakable as columns of stone. The glowing light clad him in an armour of unfading youth and set upon his head a helmet flawlessly polished and a visor with diamond eyes. At length the sun-god unfolded his whole rich crown of flaming hair with a clash of cymbals and a fanfare of trumpets; and gleams of gold shone on the boy's head.

'What is your name?' asked Robinson.

'I am called Jaan Neljapäev. I was born in Esthonia,' the boy replied, seeming to apologize for the difficult name.

'I shall call you Sunday,' said Robinson. 'It is the day of the resurrection, of the youth of all things and the day of our master, the Sun.' He added, smiling: 'To me you will always be Sunday's child.'

More about Penguins and Pelicans

Penguinews, which appears every month, contains details of all the new books issued by Penguins as they are published. From time to time it is supplemented by *Penguins in Print*, which is a complete list of all titles available. (There are some five thousand of these.)

A specimen copy of *Penguinews* will be sent to you free on request. For a year's issues (including the complete lists) please send 50p if you live in the British Isles, or 75p if you live elsewhere. Just write to Dept EP, Penguin Books Ltd, Harmondsworth, Middlesex, enclosing a cheque or postal order, and your name will be added to the mailing list.

In the U.S.A.: For a complete list of books available from Penguin in the United States write to Dept CS, Penguin Books Inc., 7110 Ambassador Road, Baltimore, Maryland 21207.

In Canada: For a complete list of books available from Penguin in Canada write to Penguin Books Canada Ltd, 41 Steelcase Road West, Markham, Ontario.

The Penguin English Library

Robinson Crusoe

Daniel Defoe
EDITED BY ANGUS ROSS

Robinson Crusoe, Defoe's first novel, was published in 1719, when that prolific master of narrative realism was almost sixty. To the majority of readers, and above all to children, the book is simply a stirring tale of shipwreck and adventure on a tropical island. By the literary historian, however, *Crusoe* can be regarded as the first English novel, and to the social historian this paean in praise of economic man offers a mine of raw material. Indeed, to quote Professor Ian Watt, '*Robinson Crusoe* falls most naturally into place, not with other novels, but with the great myths of Western civilization, with *Faust*, *Don Juan*, and *Don Quixote*'.

Flight to Arras

Antoine de Saint-Exupéry

Saint-Exupéry, a pioneer airman, is now also recognized as one of the finest modern French writers.

In *Flight to Arras* the author is sent on a reconnaissance flight over enemy-occupied France. The time is 1940, France is a shambles, his flight is pointless, and his chances of getting back alive are two to one against.

This is a classic war story about the futility of war. It is a picture of a defeated country and an understanding portrait of men who contribute to defeat by putting humanity above patriotism. And yet it is a deeply patriotic book – an explanation of how danger can change a man from pessimistic fatalism to all-seeing courage in a few seconds. It is a book in praise of man, of France, and of flying.

Also by Antoine de Saint-Exupéry
Wind, Sand and Stars

Not for sale in the U.S.A. or Canada